Snow Fury....

Snow Fury.....

By RICHARD HOLDEN

Dodd, Mead & Company
New York

For My Father and Barbara....

1 . . .

ALL OVER northern New England it had been an unusually dry summer.
And now it was early October. Along the back roads in the Western
foothills of the White Mountains the yellowing leaves were coated with
white dust. Mountain streams and even rivers had shrunk to mere trickles
amidst the sun-bleached stones of their beds, and cattle poked restlessly
at the drying mud in pasture water holes. Over the hills, already blazing
with their autumn reds and yellows, the sky had been bright and clear
for days. There was no hint of rain in the crisp, dry autumn air.

David Storm, assistant editor of the weekly *Westover Leader*, stood
by the sluiceway of the small concrete dam, looking down at the water
a good eight feet below him. "Pretty bad," he said, fingering the camera
that hung on a leather strap from his neck. He was looking at what was
left of the reservoir that supplied the town of Dixon. For some reason
the drought had hit Dixon worse than any other town in the Grafton-
Lake Sunapee region. The morning sun glinted on a mere puddle of
water, scarcely two acres in extent, surrounded by drying mud-flats.

"Bad!" The man next to him removed a shapeless felt hat and ran a
hand through his thinning white hair. "I tell you it ain't been as bad as
this in all my twenty-one years as Superintendent of the Water Works,
and you can quote me on that!" The man looked at David to see if he had
his notebook out. "The name's White," he said. "Byron C. White."

"I've got that, thanks." David glanced about the scene for a likely
picture. "So the rain-making experiment didn't pay off after all," he said.

"Rain making!" Byron C. White snorted belligerently. "Think a college professor'd have something better to do with his time than flying around in an airplane and . . . what'd he have in that little bottle anyhow?"

"Don't ask me. Silver iodide, I think. They say it's supposed to work if the conditions are right."

"Lot of damned nonsense, I say. And you can quote me on that."

"OK, Mr. White. How about standing down there and pointing to the high water mark so I can get a contrast with where the water is now." Mr. White assumed the pose with alacrity.

"You got the name," he said when David had his picture. "Byron C. White, Superintendent of Water Works twenty-one years . . ."

A few minutes later David had turned his dust-covered 1937 Chevrolet southward on the twenty-mile drive back to Westover. He had been with the *Westover Leader* less than a month, and was beginning to discover how much he liked it. He had just finished two years in the Army, and before that had worked for a public relations firm in New York. At first it had been hard to get used to the quiet tempo of both life and the news in a small college town like Westover. You got restless over endless stories of Grange and garden club meetings with their endless lists of newly elected officers. You felt like a stranger because everybody else in Westover, Dixon, Cainfield, and the other neighboring towns seemed to have lived there all their lives. But then you began to know people, and the things you wrote about began to seem more important.

On a bright autumn Saturday like this the quiet tempo of life seemed good: the morning's assignment had called for forty miles of driving through the mountains at the height of their October colors. For the afternoon, the Dixon-Westover High School football game—and no deadline until Wednesday each week. That was why he had left the city to come to New Hampshire. In New York you were like Alice's Red Queen—you had to run too hard to stay in the same place. Here one could take time to enjoy being alive. Here there was time to think—time even to think about the writing you were going to start doing some day soon.

One could do worse than settle down in Westover, he told himself.

As he drove south towards the Westover turnoff on the Dixon-Cainfield road, he noticed that the sun had grown dimmer. Ahead of him white mist obscured the upper slopes of Barker Mountain that rose just east of the road. And beyond the mountain the sky was an even misty grey.

It looked like rain and no mistake this time. He smiled to himself as he wondered if Byron C. White with his twenty-one years as Water Commissioner would be glad or disappointed. Well, rain or no rain, he would have his picture in Thursday's paper. David cranked up the side window a little and zipped up his army field jacket. Quite suddenly it had got noticeably colder.

As he neared the Westover turnoff, the grey-white clouds ahead grew thicker and seemed to dissolve into a white mist. The mist reached all the way to the ground, blotting out everything behind it, and seemed to be rolling slowly towards him. In another moment he had driven into it. He jammed on the brake in amazement. "Well, I'll be damned," he said aloud.

It was snowing.

Like other north country towns, Cainfield was used to hard winters. But even in Cainfield nobody was expecting snow as early as the second Saturday in October—not more than a passing flurry anyway. And this was no passing flurry. Heavy, soft flakes whitened the air as they sank windlessly and clung unmelting where they touched.

The windshield of the grey Willys in which Jeff Corey carried the mail for RFD #2 was already opaque with it except where the clicking wipers had cleared wet semicircles. Snow already lay thick along the road that ran north from town towards the Westover turnoff. It was thick enough so that even the tire ruts were white.

Mrs. August Gauthier, his first customer, was waiting for him by her mailbox, her hair and overcoat already powdered white.

"Snowing," he said cheerfully.

"Yes, it is." Mrs. Gauthier smiled as she took her mail. "Seems warm for snow," she added.

"Be gone by noon, I guess." Corey grinned as he shifted into gear.

Above Mrs. Gauthier's, where the Westover road turned west, a dirt road swung eastward in a slow steady climb. On the left, the road was separated from the forested slopes of Barker Mountain only by a narrow strip of field. On the right, pastureland and orchard sloped down to where, on a clear day, you could see Cainfield's red-brick clock tower and white church spires.

It was getting colder instead of warmer the way it normally should be as the morning wore on, Corey noticed. The snowflakes were smaller now, and had begun to eddy and twist over the fields in light gusts of wind. On the road ahead there were windblown patches where earth showed through, and tiny sworls of snow skittered like smoke from a cigarette. The snow was dry now, and so was the road under it. It looked now like the beginning of a blizzard. "Must be the altitude makes the difference," Corey thought.

His next stop was a row of four mailboxes at a crossroads. The mailboxes stood under a giant apple tree in front of a weathered, grey-sided farmhouse. "Gort, Bailey, Edgerton, LeBeau," Corey told himself automatically as he reached for the mail bundles with one hand, steering for the edge of the road with the other.

As he did so, the Willys gave a sudden lurch and swerved sidewise. He was able to stop the skid just short of the first mailbox. Cursing eloquently under his breath, he peered out.

Snow had piled up around a scattering of leather-skinned rotten apples in the ditch. His right front wheel had come to rest in a drift that looked, surprisingly, a good four or five inches deep. "Looks like a long winter," he told himself. Then he pulled out the mail packets for Gort, Edgerton, Bailey and LeBeau. When he looked up again, a boy about eight years old had appeared as if from nowhere out of the mist of falling snow, and stood watching him. Corey knew the boy.

"Hi, Robin," he greeted him. "Looks like good weather to make a snowman!"

"Might be," the boy said. He watched soberly as the wheels of the Willys spun futilely for a moment without gaining traction. Then, as the car disappeared down the road, he stooped down and began to pack some of the snow from the small drift together, disregarding the occasional brown apple that got mixed into the mass.

Despite its apparent dryness, the snow was sticky enough to shape. But after a few minutes his bare hands began to sting painfully. He had forgotten during the summer how cold snow could be. He pulled a pair of mittens out of his pocket and put them on.

When his ball of snow was big enough, he rolled it out of the ditch and onto the sloping lawn. It started to roll and almost got away from him. But he caught up with it halfway down the slope to the henhouse, and wedged snow under the downhill side to make it stay where it was.

In spite of the mittens, his hands hadn't stopped tingling.

A few hundred yards beyond the crossroads, Corey heard a report like a cap-pistol going off close to his ear. Under his hands the wheel pulled hard to the right, throwing the Willys into a sickening skid. It couldn't be, he thought. Not in this weather. But it was. Under the rim, his right front tire was crumpled and airless. With a sigh, he rolled up his jacket collar against the snow and went back for his jack and wrench.

By the end of the morning it had stopped snowing. The sun, still fighting through patches of cloud, had begun to burn a little of the fall off roads and southern slopes where white crests dropped soggily from still yellow goldenrod. Along Cainfield's main street, where cars and pedestrians had quickly ground the light fall to slush, there was scarcely a trace of the storm left.

In his office across from the red brick town hall, Dr. Orin Markel studied the angry welts on the palms of eight-year-old Robin Gort. "You say he got these playing in the snow?" he asked Mrs. Gort, who was hovering over her son.

She nodded. "He was making a snowball in the road without his gloves on."

"Must have scratched himself up on something," the doctor said.

"How could I?" the boy demanded. "Wasn't nothin' in the snow but old rotten apples."

"And his hands didn't begin to hurt him until later," Mrs. Gort put in.

Dr. Markel shrugged and began to rub ointment into the boy's hands.

A few blocks further down the street, Jeff Corey sat dejectedly on the steps of the grease pit in Gene Kell's service station, staring at the remains of his right front tire. "Wonder she held out as long as she did," Kell was saying. He held up the shoe and pointed to the rent. For several inches along the bottom, the rubber had been worn away to the threads.

Across the road from the Gorts' north of town, a pair of leather hunting boots stood by the door of the Edgertons' side porch. Roy Edgerton, the owner of the boots, had taken them off on the porch the evening before when he returned from a day of supervising a brush-cutting gang on the Bristol-Westover power line. During the night gusts of wind must have blown snow in onto the porch so it covered the boots. When Mrs. Edgerton spotted them later in the morning, they were still dusted with a fine white powder of snow. She picked them up to take them inside. Noticing something odd about them, she examined them more closely. When she tugged at one of the soles, it came away from the upper half way back to the instep.

The leather, where the upper had been stitched to the sole, looked as if it had been chewed by mice.

2 . . .

BOTH THE *Westover Leader* and its editor and owner, Dwight Heron, were pleasantly geared to the tempo of life in Westover. Dwight Heron seldom got to the office before ten except on Wednesdays—the day before the paper came out. His paper contented itself mostly with news of local clubs and organizations, personals, and a rambling column of the owner's called "The Heron's Perch." Spot news was left for the most part to the locally circulated dailies from Lebanon and White River Junction.

Westover, about fifteen miles west of Cainfield, was a quiet, prosperous New Hampshire town. Its principal and virtually only industry was a small men's college named Grafton.

The office of the *Leader* was in a one-story yellow brick building just off the main shopping street. It had a wide store-window front with posters of various town activities propped against the glass from inside. The offices consisted of two rooms. The front room was just large enough to handle the files and the four desks of the editorial, business and advertising staff; the back room not quite large enough for the presses, linotype machine and a pressroom crew of three.

David Storm had heard about the *Leader* and subsequently got his job as Dwight Heron's assistant through a friend in New York who knew Dwight and had worked with him on the paper when he first bought it eight years before. The other members of the editorial (business and advertising) staff included Heron's wife, Gloria, a plump, fortyish woman, who appeared in the office often enough to handle most of the weekly club and organizational news, and a slight, grey-haired, taciturn woman named Mrs. Bigelow, who did most of the secretarial work and accounts.

It was almost half past eleven when David parked his car in the empty lot behind the *Leader* building. It was still cold, but there had been no snow in Westover. The sky was misty but cloudless, and the sun shone brightly in the yellow leaves of the elms along the streets.

Dwight was alone at his desk in the office as David came in. "Snowing in Cainfield," he said casually as he unzipped his field jacket. Dwight looked up.

"Lucky I just heard it on the radio," he said. "Otherwise I would strongly suspect you needed to change your brand of whiskey."

In the few weeks David had been working for the *Leader* he had already become close friends with Dwight Heron. Heron, plump and benevolent-looking with his tousled sandy hair, moon-face and contagious good humor, was the kind of man who knew and liked everyone in town. Consequently he was known and liked by everyone in return. With these qualifications and nothing more, David thought, he would have made a perfect editor of the *Westover Leader*. What's more, he was a thoroughly good guy and easy to work for.

"Really snowing hard?" Dwight asked.

"Could hardly see the road in front of me. Then, a couple of miles west of the corner, I was out of it as suddenly as I'd come into it. Couple of miles more and the sun was shining."

"That's the funny thing," Dwight said. "According to the radio it isn't snowing or even raining anywhere around except within a five-mile radius of the town of Cainfield. Well, that's New Hampshire weather for you. If you don't like the way it is now, just wait a minute. You get your pictures up in Dixon OK?"

"Sure did—complete with Byron C. White, twenty-one years Superintendent of the Water Works. You know," David sat down on the desk facing Dwight's, "it's sort of too bad this snowstorm didn't land on the good Mr. White up in Dixon. Might have made him less sceptical of Professor Cruickshank's rain-making efforts."

"Guess he's grateful enough to Cruickshank as it is for the free publicity. You want to go back over to Cainfield this afternoon and get a couple of pictures?"

"Thought I was covering the ball game this afternoon."

"Forget about it. Our boy from the Westover High paper will take care of that for us."

"What sort of pictures you want? Season's first snowball fight and stuff like that?"

"Sure, or a couple of St. Bernards warming up. Anything you can find. If you get some good ones we can do a spread. Maybe tie it in with your Dixon drought pictures." Heron took out his pipe and a yellow oilskin tobacco pouch. "You know, Dave, I've been thinking about this Cruickshank angle. You ever met Professor Cruickshank?"

"Nope. I know he's an old friend of yours, that's all. You're the one who saw him about the cloud-seeding story last week. Why? You think his rain making might have started the snow in Cainfield?"

Poker-faced, Heron shrugged. "Might be an angle." He chuckled suddenly. "Like to pin it on him if I could. Jesus, he'd be so Goddam mad!" He savored the idea in silence for a moment or two. "If it snows enough to make it a really freak storm for the time of year, he'll probably get blamed for it anyway. We might as well make a good thing of it—Grafton biochemistry professor thinks he can cure Dixon water shortage by cloud-seeding. Tries all fall to get permission to do it. Finally does get permission. Hires a plane and dumps his carbon dioxide or whatever it is right spang over the Dixon reservoir. What happens? Within five miles of the Dixon reservoir absolutely nothing—maybe even a little dryer than it was before. But just three days later, Cainfield, seven miles to the south, has its own special snowstorm. . . ." He fell to chuckling silently again. "You might go over and see the professor anyway."

David looked at him half-smiling. "You serious, Dwight?"

Heron lifted himself laboriously out of his chair. "Oh, I'm always serious." He lumbered across the room to get a match out of his jacket which was on a coat-rack in the corner. "Professor's got a very nice daughter, by the way."

David decided at once Heron was right about Professor Cruickshank's daughter. The girl who opened the door was very pleasant to look at, even in blue jeans and paint-smeared woolen T-shirt. She was about five or six years younger than he was, David decided—not more than twenty-five. Her light brown hair was straight and cut fairly short. Her eyes were large and very grey, with surprisingly dark lashes. And there was a boyish frankness about her smile as he introduced himself. "I'm Karen Cruickshank," she said. "Come on in and don't mind the costume. I was just painting a bookcase." She wiped her paint-stained hands on her jeans. "Dwight Heron and Dad have known each other for years. Funny I haven't met you before."

"My misfortune," David said.

"I suppose you want to see Dad." She went to the foot of the stairs and looked back at him. "More about cloud-seeding?"

Under her straightforward glance, David suddenly felt a little embarrassed about the reason for his visit. "Well, I suppose it could be," he said. "You see, it seems to be snowing in Cainfield."

"Snowing?" She looked genuinely surprised for a minute, and then laughed suddenly. "And you think Dad . . . ? Oh, come on, now! Dad may be the best and only amateur rain maker in the county. But he isn't that good!"

She turned and called upstairs. Professor Cruickshank came down almost immediately. He was a tall, athletic fifty. His lean, angular face was deeply tanned under iron-grey hair. From behind thick-lensed glasses, his eyes met David's with what looked like unblinking coldness as Karen performed the introductions. "So you're the new fellow who's working with Dwight, eh?" he said.

"This gentleman seems to think you've started a snowstorm in Cainfield," Karen explained.

"You flatter me," the professor said, shaking hands with David. "You say it's snowing in Cainfield? Well, it won't be the first time it's snowed so early hereabouts. I remember it snowed in July once some years ago."

"I think the reason Mr. Storm is here, Dad," Karen explained, "is to ask if you think your cloud-seeding experiments up at Dixon could have had anything to do with it." Both Karen and her father turned and looked at David expectantly.

"*Is* that what you wanted to ask me?" The professor smiled slightly. David felt increasingly uncomfortable.

"Well," he began, "what I meant was . . ."

"The answer is no," the professor said. "It is an interesting idea, though. Hardly likely—in fact quite impossible. But interesting, nonetheless." He walked to the window and looked out. "How hard is it snowing in Cainfield? Do you have any idea?" David told him his experience on the road back from Dixon. "You say the snow seemed dry? It was staying on the ground?" The professor turned back from the window. An amused smile twisted his mouth. "I suppose this is some joke of Dwight's to send you over here and ask me if I'm responsible. Well, you can tell Dwight I'll give him an exclusive on some secret experiments of mine—a deadly nerve gas which is quite harmless to everybody except editors of small-town papers. You aren't by any chance going back to Cainfield, are you?"

"Yes," David said. "I'm on my way there now."

"Oh, really? I wish I could go with you. I've made sort of a study of weather in an amateurish sort of way, and I'm always interested in freak storms like this."

"Why don't you come along, then," David said. "Perhaps your daughter'd like to come too?" He looked inquiringly at Karen, who, in turn, looked at her father.

Cruickshank seemed suddenly lost in his thoughts. "I'd like to go," he said. "Really wish I could. But there's nothing to prevent Karen from going. Might be a good idea if she did—since I seem to have such a personal connection with this snowstorm of yours . . ." His voice trailed off, and after some hesitation he turned, and with a casual wave in David's direction, went back upstairs. Karen stared after him thoughtfully for a moment. Then she turned to David.

"Don't mind Dad," she said. "He's writing something at the moment—some sort of paper on an experiment he's in the midst of—not the poison gas for editors, or even assistant editors." She laughed. "And he gets like that when he's preoccupied—just wanders off. Once when we were visiting some friends for dinner, and he was in the midst of something like this, he forgot he wasn't home and just wandered upstairs and took a bath." She laughed again.

"Real absent-minded professor," David said. Karen was nervous about something, he thought. So was her father. "*You're* coming with me, aren't you?" he asked.

"If you really want me to, I'd love to. Can you wait while I change?"

"I can't believe I'm going to need all this," Karen said as she climbed into the seat of David's ancient Chevrolet. She was wearing a trenchcoat, and was busy tying a bright-colored scarf around her head. The sun was still bright, and the air somewhat above freezing as they turned into the winding blacktop road that led out of Westover. But over the mountains to the east ahead of them lay a bank of soot-grey cloud.

"You got sort of railroaded into taking me along," Karen went on. "Hope you don't mind."

"Couldn't have worked out better," David said, smiling at her. "Don't be too sure I won't try to get a story out of you though."

"As payment for the lift? Well, you may try."

"For instance, correct me if I am wrong, but your father seemed tremendously interested, and also a little upset about the snow in Cainfield. There isn't any chance his cloud-seeding *could* have had anything to do with it, is there?"

"You're very observant, aren't you?" she said. "But the answer is still no. I told you Dad is that way sometimes. He's working right now on some very complicated research—all very technical and hush-hush. I don't know what it's all about. But he doesn't like publicity because of it, I guess. He was a little miffed at Dwight for running the story about the cloud-seeding in the first place."

"Why? Did that have anything to do with what he's working on?"

"No. Dad just had a bug in his ear about the cloud-seeding, I guess." She looked at him suddenly, her grey eyes serious. "You know the only reason I am telling you any of this is because you work for Dwight. I know he wouldn't print anything Dad didn't want him to."

"I wouldn't print anything you told me not to either."

"No, I don't think you would. I didn't mean to suggest that. But I'd lay off the whole thing if I were you."

They were both silent a few minutes. "Dad's onto something big, I think," she said at last. "He can't talk about it. And yet, I can see it has him worried. He even seems to be afraid of something."

"What exactly is he afraid of?"

"I couldn't tell you if I knew," she said. She fell silent again. The car sped on towards the bank of cloud in the east. "But I don't know."

"The funny thing is," she added, "I don't think he knows either."

3...

About four miles outside of Cainfield the weather changed abruptly. The sun disappeared behind clouds the color of smoke from a soft-coal burning factory. Thin patches of snow began to appear along the sides of the road in places where the withering grass was shortest. Where the road went through steep cuts, the exposed yellow sand of the slopes was still powdered with clinging white. It had stopped snowing. But, as they neared Cainfield, the surrounding fields began to look whiter. There were evidences of slush still on the smooth black surface of the road. The air was noticeably cooler.

David slowed down as they drove up to a crossroads. "Mind if we take the north road?" he asked. "Little longer, but there might be a better chance for some pictures."

"It's your expedition," Karen said. "Didn't know you were a photographer too."

"Didn't know I was either till I sank some back pay in a camera when I got out of the Army. You get to be a little of everything on a country paper."

"You aren't from around here, are you?" she asked.

"No," he said, "I don't know where I'm from exactly. Family lives in New York. I worked there before I was in the Army. But I don't seem to like it there any more. I'd like to be from somewhere. But I guess all I can say is I live in Westover at the moment."

"You say you're a veteran?"

"Hm-m. Drafted. Nothing spectacular."

"Does it have to be spectacular?" He took his eyes from the road a moment to look at her. Her hair stuck out in silky brown wisps from under her scarf, and in profile her face looked softer and less boyish.

"No, I suppose not," he said. "I suppose you wonder what I'm doing in Westover?"

"I presumed you were working for the *Westover Leader*," she said, fishing a cigarette out of the pocket of her trenchcoat. "What sort of pictures you looking for?"

"Oh, just snow pictures," he said, twisting the wheel sharply to avoid a rut in the dirt road they had been following since the crossroads. The road was bare and brown now, and a little wet. But on either side the cleared fields were white.

"What's the matter with that?" she asked finally. They were approaching another crossroads with four mailboxes under an old apple tree. On the white lawn between the road and a bleak, grey-clapboard farmhouse stood a large snowball, about half the height of a small boy. "Why not get the boy who made that to pose with it?"

She had something, David thought. He pulled the car into the almost snowless ditch.

Mrs. Gort was reluctant. "Robin hurt his hands playing with something in the snow this morning . . . and he's all dressed up to go visiting right now. We're leaving in a few minutes." The sound of a car starting from behind the far corner of the house confirmed her haste. But Robin, in a correct grey flannel suit and plaid cap, was finally permitted to oblige on condition he didn't get himself "into the snow."

He showed the bandages on his palms under his wool mittens, and then posed with one mittened hand on the snowball. "It's got lots bigger since this morning," he said as David made preliminary adjustments on his camera.

"Guess you must have been working on it," David said.

"Nope." The boy smoothed the top of the snowball affectionately. "Got bigger all by itself."

"Where did you find all the snow to build such a big snowball?" Karen wanted to know. As she spoke, she leaned down and scooped some snow from the lawn with her bare hands. It was scarcely half an inch deep.

"In the ditch over there where your car is," the boy said. "Ain't much there now, but there was plenty this morning."

"There's a story for you," Karen said as they drove off. "Little boy's snowball gets bigger all by itself." Her hands were still wet from the snow. She rubbed them together to warm them. "Did you ever make snowballs like that when you were little?"

"Not many, I guess. I was a city boy."

"I grew up on it," she said. "And I still think there's something exciting about a first snow. What if his snowball really did get bigger?"

"In that case your father might have to answer some very embarrassing questions."

"I suppose he might!" Karen laughed silently. Then she grew suddenly thoughtful. "Kidding aside," she said, "where did he get the snow to make that snowball? I've made some like it, and it takes an awful lot of snow."

"I was thinking of that," David said. "It would have had to snow most of the night."

"Who knows? Maybe it did."

"That's the funniest part of it," David said. "I had to go up to Dixon this morning. I passed the Westover corner, two or three miles from here, about nine o'clock. It was a little cloudy, I guess, but it wasn't snowing, and it hadn't been snowing. Not there anyway. It was only on my way back at about eleven that I ran into the snow."

"That doesn't mean it couldn't have started snowing much earlier where we are now. You don't know New Hampshire weather the way I do."

"No, but I'm learning." David felt vaguely dissatisfied with this explanation. But it was a silly thing to spend time worrying about. He smiled. "I'm afraid you're right," he said. "It must have got bigger all by itself."

Osbert L. Carmichael, Cainfield's ruddy-faced police Chief, grinned in recognition as David entered the one-room police headquarters at the back of the town hall. "Got something real hot for you this morning," he said. "It snowed."

"That's what I heard," David said. The Chief's face crinkled into an exaggerated frown as he picked up a thin sheaf of papers. "Other than that," he said, "one drunken driving, one yellow-line violation—hell, you don't go to press till Tuesday!"

"Thought you might have something on the snow."

"Such as what? Just weather to us—at least till someone skids into a phone pole."

"Any idea when it started snowing?"

Carmichael thought a moment. "Heard some people live north of town say it started about two or three o'clock in the morning. Other places around didn't get so much. Seems to have been a Cainfield special. We seem to be the only town that got it—and not all places even in Cainfield got it the same."

"I noticed that," David said. "Seems to be particularly heavy up the back road towards Barker Mountain."

"Up by Gorts and Edgertons?"

"I guess so."

"Heard it was bad up that way. Roy Edgerton was in this morning. Said there was sort of a freak wind around his place last night. Woke him up. Said he never saw the snow coming down so thick. Be gone by night, though, I guess."

Gene Kell at the service station down the street didn't have much to offer. David had already marked Kell as a good source for such spot news as accidents or general gossip around Cainfield. He usually bought a few gallons of gas from him each time he passed through to cement relations. But this time all he got was five gallons of regular.

"Nobody's ever surprised to see it snow around here—even this early in October," Kell said as he wiped David's windshield. "Can't say I mind it, either. I can start moving some knobbies if it keeps up. Looks like it would too." The sky had darkened again, and scattered flakes were already falling.

The selectmen's office in the town hall, where David thought he might get an idea of what Cainfield was planning to do in the way of emergency snow clearance, echoed the town's general apathy towards so slight and so early a fall. Everybody was out to lunch.

It was twelve-thirty by the clock on the town hall tower as David came out of the selectmen's office and rejoined Karen in the car. "Don't suppose you'd have lunch with me?" he asked.

Karen smiled. "Don't suppose I have any choice," she said. "Doesn't take you long to fall into the New Hampshire idiom," she added as they crossed the street from the parking corridor to the Waverton Hotel Grill, "always asking questions in the negative. Why shouldn't I have lunch with you?"

"I don't know. It's a long time since anyone has. This all right?"

"You know of any other place to eat in Cainfield?"

The Waverton Grill was the kind of New Hampshire dining-room less distinguished for its cuisine than for the fact it was the only place in town where you could legally order a mixed drink. The funereal expanse of white-clothed tables was almost empty. The waitress, a weary-looking middle-aged woman in a pale green cotton uniform, took their order and brought their martinis grudgingly, as if implying disapproval of people who ate and drank in public restaurants.

As she handed them the menus, she invalidated them with the explanation that the cook was sick and that there was a choice of pot-roast or scallops—"only we're out of scallops," she explained.

"Glad you aren't out of pot-roast," David said. Then he looked at Karen over his martini glass. He hadn't really had a chance to look at her since he had first seen her in the paint-stained T-shirt. She looked very different now in a cool-looking navy-blue sweater, her tawny hair combed smooth and held back above the temple with a silver clip.

"Is it really so long since you've had lunch with anyone?" she asked.

"With anyone like you."

She smiled. "Well, you got what ought to be a cute picture anyway. Sorry the angle with Dad about the snowstorm turned out to be a frost. But I'm glad I came along anyway." She looked at him quizzically. "How do you find it being on a small town paper? A little dull? I imagine you would for a while."

He looked down at his martini. "No, not dull. It's good to be in a place for a change where nothing special is happening. A snowstorm out of season and who cares? Nothing ever changes around here except the usual run of births, marriages and deaths."

Karen shrugged. "Well, that covers a lot of territory—births, marriages and deaths. What else happens anywhere that's really important? What else causes most of the happiness and unhappiness in the world—even in this out-of-the-way corner of New Hampshire?"

"Well, other things do happen," he said. "It's a pretty small world these days, and things can happen halfway across the globe that affect us here. Maybe one shouldn't run away to a small town and hide from it."

"Hide from it? What do you think the rest of the world is mostly except small towns like this one—each with its births, marriages and deaths —and unimportant snowstorms. After all, that's what life's made of."

David picked up his drink. "I guess I can't argue that. Anyway, here I am, covering an unimportant snowstorm."

Karen started to answer, but somebody had stopped by their table. He was a short, slight man in a tweed coat and plaid, tieless shirt. He hesitated a moment on the point of recognizing David. "You're Dick Storm, aren't you?" he asked finally.

"David Storm," David corrected. With an inward groan he recognized the man in tweeds as someone named something like Manning, who worked for the state biological survey in the state capitol at Concord. Manning was someone he had happened to meet and talk to while working up at Dixon the week before on the drought story.

Manning accepted David's reluctant invitation, and pulled up an extra chair. With scarcely a nod towards Karen in answer to David's introduction, he began at once to talk about his present mission in Cainfield. Seems that microtus (the common field mouse, he explained) was in the habit of nibbling the bark off of young fruit trees. He had been sent by Concord on a routine check of local microtus damage. The unseasonable snow didn't help, he pointed out, since the ravages of microtus were less easily traceable when there was snow on the ground. His discourse, virtually a monologue, was interrupted by the waitress, who had a call for David—from Westover, she said.

"Dwight, no doubt," David said as he rose. "Wonder how he knew I'd be here." His face was troubled as he returned from the phone booth. "Your father called Dwight, Karen," he said. "Wanted to know if he knew where we were. He wants you to come home as soon as you can. It's important."

It was Karen's turn to look puzzled. "Anything wrong?"

"Don't think it's anything serious. Wants you to come home, though. Something's come up."

"Oh, David, I'm sorry." The microtus man, who had reluctantly halted his story, rose with a hesitant smile and took his departure. He looked, David thought, as if he believed the phone call had been a deliberate plant to get rid of him. David and Karen rose. Beyond the window, David noticed, the street once again was almost blind with falling snow.

In the car Karen sat with her fists thrust deep into the pockets of her trenchcoat as David sped the Chevrolet back towards Westover through the wind-driven flakes of the new fall. "I've spoiled your story," she said. "If this new snow amounts to anything, you could stay over here and have a story."

"Births, marriages and deaths and small snowstorms," he quoted her. "Besides, we don't go to press until Tuesday."

"Especially sorry about lunch," she said.

"So am I. Can we do it again?"

"I'd like it."

"Look, what about your father? Anything wrong, you think?"

"Don't think so."

"Anything I can do?"

"Nothing to do anything about. You can call me if you feel like it." She hesitated as she got out of the car in front of her house. "I suppose I could get in touch with you if I needed to?"

He gave her his number. He lived in a room on the second floor of a boarding house near the center of town. But, being on the paper, he already had his own phone.

"Thanks," she said, taking the slip of paper he handed her. "Thanks for everything." She gave him a sudden searching look, then hurried up the steps to the house. Once on the steps she hesitated and turned back. Then she went in quickly and closed the door.

The snowball on the lawn of the Gort place outside of Cainfield stood on its precarious slope above the henhouse, a little to one side of the main farm dwelling. The snow that had started again in the afternoon swirled around it for hours without disturbing its equilibrium. But along about four o'clock, it edged a little downhill.

Finally, a few minutes after it had first moved, it became topheavy at last, slipped its mooring, and rolled the rest of the way down the slope to the henhouse. It fetched up against the wire and plank siding with a dull "chunk."

On impact the snowball exploded into loose fragments. The explosion scarcely disturbed the occupants of the henhouse—eighteen barred plymouth rock hens. And for some time after, there was no sound except the occasional sighing of the wind around the corner of the henhouse.

The exploded snowball was at first an ungainly heap. Then, finally, as the wind smoothed it, it became a gracefully sloping mound against the side of the henhouse. It wasn't cold, scarcely more than freezing. But the top of the mound stirred in the wind like curling smoke, and whispered like falling sand.

As darkness fell, the snow began to filter into the henhouse through the loose planking and chickenwire. It sifted slowly at first, and then at last tumultuously, as water finds its way through the widening flaws of a dyke.

At first the sleepy plymouth rocks paid little attention. But finally their nervous clucking grew into a cacophony of squawking which anyone at the Gort farmhouse would have heard if they hadn't been away visiting relatives.

Then, after a while, it was still again, except for the sandlike whisper of windblown snow.

4 ...

AFTER HE HAD dropped Karen off, David drove back to the *Leader* office, parking his car in an alley around back of the building as he had learned to do during business hours when Westover's parking meters demanded five cents an hour. The sun had gone, he noticed, and the sky was pearly grey. But, as yet, no snow had fallen in Westover.

"What's up with Karen's father?" David asked as he came into the office, which ordinarily would have been deserted on Saturday afternoon. Dwight was seated at his desk, pouring over a geological survey map. Mrs. Bigelow frowned over his shoulder, the light gleaming on her spectacles.

"Don't know any more than I told you over the phone," Dwight said without looking up from the map. "Just something important came up, I guess, and he wanted to talk with her about it." He glanced up. "We're invited over there for dinner tonight, by the way."

"We?"

"Yep, you too. Can you make it?"

David smiled. "I think I can squeeze it in. You know it's snowing again over there."

"I know. It's on the radio. WDSV in Claremont just picked it up on the afternoon news. You know this is the damndest snowstorm—Mrs. Bigelow's been calling up. Few flurries in Dixon, northwest, and a few as far south as Cainfield Center. Nothing here, and no snow east of Barker Mountain on the other side. Not a single flake anywhere, further than five miles from Cainfield. What do you make of it, Dave?"

David shrugged. "You're the expert on New Hampshire weather. Anyhow, I guess we can't connect it up with the professor and his cloud-seeding."

"Well, I didn't think you could, really. Nobody's ever proved cloud-seeding could produce rain—let alone snow. But people might start tying him up with it—especially if the storm stays local and gets really big. Thought we might as well too. What did he say?"

"He was kind of funny about it as a matter of fact. Think he got a little sore. Sent Karen along with me to take a look, but didn't want to go himself."

Dwight grinned. "I guess that was tough. Don't mind the professor, though, if he gets like that. He's a wonderful guy. I've known him a long time. He's just a little sensitive about this cloud-seeding business because he knows people don't take it seriously. He never has liked publicity either. He's even gone so far as to fix up a little shack out in the woods over near Dixon somewhere with a lot of laboratory equipment. He likes to disappear up there weekends and do his own research where no one can bother him. Makes a big secret of it. Guess most people don't even know where the shack is."

"What exactly is he doing up there? From what Karen says, it sounds like something rather big."

Dwight leaned back in his chair and started poking at the bowl of his pipe with an already ash-stained finger. "When a guy as far up the ladder in the biochemistry field as he is does research in his spare time, he probably isn't just playing around with a kid's chemocraft set. I don't think he's inventing a new kind of atom bomb or anything like that. But . . ."

"I wouldn't be too sure about that," Mrs. Bigelow said. "I've got a grand-nephew who has one of those toy chemistry sets. He's been trying to make a hydrogen bomb out of it ever since last Christmas."

"Any luck?" Dwight asked her.

"Give him time, give him time." Mrs. Bigelow walked over towards her desk. "I'll be running along now if you don't need me any more."

"No, you go ahead, Mrs. B. David and I'll probably be running back to Cainfield to look around if it keeps on snowing. Nothing else to do around here though. See you Monday, and don't forget to put up your storm windows!"

"Karen seems to think her father's worried about something," David said later as he sat next to Dwight in the front seat of the latter's car on the way back to Cainfield.

"Guess most of us are worried about *something*," Dwight said. "Nice girl, isn't she?"

"Karen?" David nodded. "Uh-huh."

"To tell the truth," Dwight went on, "I know damned well he's worried about something. But I don't know what, and I don't think it's any of my business. Don't think it has anything to do with the snow in Cainfield, though. If you ask me there's absolutely nothing behind that snowstorm but the plain natural cussedness of New Hampshire weather."

Cainfield hadn't yet taken its snow very seriously. One of the town's two snowplows was in the midst of repairs. But there wasn't enough snow yet to require the services of the one that functioned. Gene Kell at the service station had to answer a call from someone who was stuck on the Cainfield Center road. But the trouble turned out to be a faulty ignition rather than snow. The fire department had had two chimney fires since noon. Both of them could have been attributed to the snow, since they were caused by fires which might not have been lighted or banked so high if the weather had been more seasonable. But on the fire department's books the cause was more likely dirty flues. And the state police had a minor collision on their hands when a car had skidded into a lumber truck a mile south of town. This too could have been caused by the snow. But the police were more interested in the fact that the driver of the car smelled of alcohol.

It was too late for the snow to cause any crop damages. And the fall was neither deep enough yet to be a serious obstruction, nor was it slippery enough to have caused any accidents in which anyone was hurt. The most impressive thing about the storm was that it was a surprisingly good one for so early in October. Nobody except Luther Angus, who was eighty-four and had lived in Cainfield longer than anyone else alive, could remember when there had ever been so much snow so early. And a certain amount of civic pride attached to the fact that this time the storm was geographically Cainfield's own and nobody else's. The beer drinkers at the counter in Wendell's Cafe were even thicker than usual on a Saturday afternoon as more and more radio news reports gave Cainfield and its snow a passing mention.

David took some more pictures. And when they got back to the office in Westover late in the afternoon, Dwight decided to take a chance on sending some of them, including the earlier one of the snowball, in to one of the press services in Boston on the five o'clock bus.

After that David went home to his bedroom-kitchen apartment off Main Street to get dressed for dinner at the Cruickshanks'. He was a little puzzled at being asked on such short notice. But it was a pleasant surprise to be going out to dinner. He knew very few people in Westover yet except the Herons and the people he met in the line of business.

It was especially pleasant to be going to the Cruickshanks', because Karen would be there.

Professor Cruickshank had been a widower for ten years, David learned from Dwight on the way over. He lived alone with his daughter and taught several courses at Grafton, where he was head of the Biochemistry Department. He was better off than most professors, having a private income, independent of his teacher's salary. Karen, since she had graduated from Radcliffe College in Cambridge three years before, had stayed in Westover to be with her father, and worked as a retoucher in a photographer's shop in town to keep busy.

The Cruickshanks' house, David noticed more carefully than he had on his first visit that morning, was a pleasantly remodelled New England colonial with white shingles and green shutters. It was enough like the other houses on the street to harmonize with them, but enough different to have its own distinct personality.

Karen met them at the door in a pale blue cocktail dress that made her look much smaller and slenderer than when David had first seen her that morning.

"The gentlemen of the press," she said, smiling at David and pecking Dwight on the cheek. Then she led them to a living-room, lined to the ceiling with bookshelves. Professor Cruickshank rose from an armchair, setting aside a spring binder that had been open on his knee. His face looked drawn, but this time he smiled cordially as they entered.

"I hope Mr. Storm didn't think I was too rude this morning," he said. "But I'm very glad you both could come, Dwight. And this time I have a particular reason."

Later, after Karen had brought in martini fixings on a tray and set them in front of her father for mixing and distributing, the talk swung inevitably to the Cainfield snowstorm. "Still going on hard as ever according to the four o'clock news," the professor said, staring at his glass.

"Was when we left a little before that," Dwight said.

"So you did go back?" Karen glanced up at David. "Sorry I had to pull you away from it earlier, but . . ." Her glance shifted from David's chair to her father's.

Her father set down his glass. "That brings up something," he began. "I said I had a reason for asking you gentlemen over tonight. I have. I know you can keep a confidence, Dwight. I'm sure you both can." His glance included David. "Well, I told Mr. Storm something this morning . . ."

"About the cloud-seeding?" David asked.

The professor nodded. "Can I be sure this is off the record? It won't go any further than us?"

"Of course, Nathan. What's up?" Dwight sat up in his chair, his eyes kindling with interest.

"Well, what I told Mr. Storm this morning wasn't true."

Dwight sat up still further. "Good God, man! You mean you think there really is a connection between the Cainfield storm and your damned cloud-seeding?"

The professor drained his martini. "I'm afraid it's quite possible. More than possible. You see, after Mr. Storm left with Karen this morning, several other newspaper people called me up and asked if there was a connection. I denied it, of course—told them the same thing I told Mr. Storm. I had hoped the snow would prove only a flurry—that it would not be necessary to mention a possible connection. It can be a mistake, you know, to let that kind of a cat out of the bag until there is some kind of scientific proof. But when people as far away as the Rutland *Post* and the Manchester *Globe-Democrat* began to call about it, I found myself in rather a dilemma. So I thought I had better tell you about it, Dwight—and you, too, Mr. Storm, in all fairness after the misinformation I gave you. When I called Karen back this afternoon, she quite agreed that it was best to tell you."

"You make it all sound rather ominous, Nathan," Dwight said. "After all, it's only a snowstorm. Besides, how can you be so sure your cloud-seeding had anything to do with it? After all has it ever been conclusively proved that seeding has caused a single drop of rain that wouldn't have fallen anyway?"

"Almost conclusively, I should say. And I'm beginning to be afraid I may have started something more than I bargained for."

"How do you mean?" David asked. "Was your cloud-seeding any different from the usual thing?"

"Well, yes, it was in a way." The professor picked up the shaker and crossed the room to fill the other glasses. "I don't know whether Karen has told you, Mr. Storm, but I have a laboratory where I often go weekends—back in the woods near Barker Mountain. That's between Dixon and Cainfield. I do some experimenting up there, the nature of which is neither here nor there—but it could have rather important results. One of the by-products of what I was doing was some snow crystals with rather unusual properties. For one thing, these laboratory crystals of mine had a remarkably strong affinity for moisture. . . ."

He smiled a little tensely as he sat down again and filled his own glass. "That probably sounds ridiculous to you—a snow crystal with an affinity of its own for moisture. I was able to establish that, however—it was due to certain impurities.

"But you can see where that leads. That's what got me interested in the cloud-seeding experiment. I wanted to try combining some of my crystals with the frozen silver iodide ordinarily used in such experiments on the idea they might have an effect on the normal cloud vapor in the atmosphere." He smiled wistfully. "Well, I finally did try it. And I'm afraid what is happening in Cainfield may be the result."

"Well, I'll be damned!" Dwight said. "So that's what you've been up to?"

"Sounds as if you might have hit on something rather important," David said. "But why the secrecy?"

"Well, that may be an unnecessary precaution. I hope so."

"What Dad's worried about," Karen put in, "is that if it turned out to be a bad storm in Cainfield, and people know Dad had—well, sort of a hand in it—it might prejudice people against doing anything further with a very important discovery. And, of course, Dad hasn't proved yet to what extent the storm actually was caused by his crystals—if it was at all. All he knows is what the crystals do in the lab."

"My daughter's putting it very mildly," the professor said. "What I'm worried about is, well—if my crystals are to blame for the storm—I don't know how long it's going to go on snowing in Cainfield."

Karen looked at him, her eyes widening. "You didn't tell me that, Dad—you mean it could go *on* and *on?*"

The professor avoided her eyes. "If my crystals actually did cause the storm, then that's a possibility, yes."

Dwight whistled. "You mean it just wouldn't stop?"

"Well, certain weather changes could interrupt it eventually. I don't really know. You see, the possibility, though calculable, was so fantastic. . ."

Dwight shook his head slowly. "Fantastic is no word for it! Nathan, are you sure you know what you're talking about?"

"I hope it turns out that I don't."

"Let's try the radio!" Karen said. She jumped from her chair and went to the console against the wall. David followed her, and the others drifted over as blurps of music and static began to come from the set under Karen's fingers. Finally a newscaster was talking about riots in Czechoslovakia, then: "In Cainfield, New Hampshire, more than two inches of snow have fallen since the earliest hours of this morning. Not only was the Cainfield storm, which ended as skies began to clear at four-thirty this afternoon, an all-time record for the second week in October in the area, but no snow whatever has been reported from any locality in that part of the state further than ten miles from Cainfield. Attributing the storm to freak atmospheric currents in the mountain region, Boston's veteran Chief Meteorologist, Francis X. Hallihan, said the storm definitely could not be attributed to radiation from recent H-bomb tests in the Pacific." Karen snapped the set off and straightened up, turning to her father with a sigh.

"It's stopped, Dad."

Her father's face looked suddenly less strained. He laid a hand on Dwight's shoulder. "I think now I begin to feel a little more like dinner."

Down the road from the Gort's place, north of Cainfield, sixty-year-old John Bailey stood in the lighted doorway of his side porch and looked out across the snow-covered field that stretched dimly from his yard to the Gort's back fence. The stars were out again after the snow, but there was no moon, and it was too dark to see very far. "Here, Fox!" he called. "Here, Fox, good boy, come here now!" But the sudden yelping that had brought him to his door had ceased. As far out on the field as he could see, there was no sign of Fox, who was a large collie. Only circles of tracks in the dooryard.

Bailey went back into the house to get his boots and windbreaker. He picked up a lantern and his .32 special carbine and started out into the snow. The way Fox had yelped, it sounded like porcupine, though you

[27]

wouldn't expect to find a porcupine out there in the open field. Could have been a wildcat. He held the lantern high and circled till he found where the collie's tracks led out of the yard into the field.

He buttoned his collar tighter against the slight but cold wind and called again. But there was no answering bark, and no movement in the pale whiteness ahead as far as his lantern permitted him to see. Or was there a movement? The corner of his eye caught something brighter than the snow that seemed to shift at the furthest limit of his vision. He stepped forward more quickly. But the snow was deeper here, and walking was not so easy as it had been in the yard.

The snow had drifted a good deal out here in the open. He nearly stumbled once, and cursed in surprise as his foot sank in unexpectedly well above the knee. There was more wind than he had expected. The snow was dry and still drifting a little. In the silence, as he paused to listen between increasingly difficult steps, it made a soft, sandy noise as it stirred. The snow looked very bright under the stars and something was definitely moving now, just ahead. He raised his lantern and stepped forward, opening his mouth to call Fox again. Instead he uttered only a strangled whimper of terror . . .

Lying on its side in the snow, the kerosene lantern guttered smokily for a few minutes, and then went out, leaving the stars bright again over the pale, whispering whiteness.

5 . . .

AFTER DINNER at the Cruickshanks' house that evening, Dwight and the professor sat in front of the fire over coffee, while David, at Karen's suggestion, helped her with the dishes in the kitchen.

After the news that it had stopped snowing in Cainfield, the professor had suddenly became more cheerful and steered away from the subject of the snow. At dinner he had even got onto one of his favorite leisure-time topics of conversation—the origin of the unique species of golden trout found nowhere else in the world except in nearby Lake Sunapee. And Dwight did all he could to keep the conversation on golden trout and other topics far removed from snow, cloud-seeding and biochemistry in general. The professor looked very tired, he thought.

It wasn't until after dinner over the coffee that Dwight's curiosity finally got the better of him. "Nathan, what in hell made you think it was going to go on snowing indefinitely in Cainfield? That is what you were afraid of, isn't it? Do you really have something that could cause a thing like that?"

The professor thought for a moment in silence. "I was afraid it was barely possible, Dwight. And if it happened, I would have been very seriously to blame. I should have studied my crystals a good deal further in the lab before attempting any experiments with them that might have caused harm to others. I can't forgive myself for taking such a chance. Just got carried away, I'm afraid. But fortunately it did stop snowing. The least I can do now is to keep my secret so that no other damned fools can tinker with it and cause trouble."

"You really believe such a thing is possible, then—a sort of self-per-petuating snowstorm?"

"Who knows what is possible and what isn't, Dwight? We know that all matter obeys certain laws. But as yet we know very few of the laws. We know, for example, that a crystal always assumes the same shape— a snow crystal is always hexagonal. And we can measure the angles of a crystal's planes, and know that in any given substance they never vary a fraction of a degree. But do we know why? Nothing we know about the atom or molecular structure as yet tells us that. The 'why' of a crystal's structure is as mysterious as the 'why' of life itself. Until we know the answer to these 'why's' we cannot know what even so simple a fragment of matter as a snow crystal is capable of under certain stresses and in-fluences. And we must experiment with caution because we cannot al-ways know what kind of a genie will come out of our bottle."

"You aren't going on with your experiments, then?"

"I didn't say that. But if it has really stopped snowing in Cainfield, then it fortunately won't be necessary for me to make them public. I can wait now until I am sure of my answers and know what it is I've stumbled onto." He looked at Dwight with a queer half-smile. "I'm still almost afraid of what I may find."

In the kitchen Karen did the dishes while David dried. "Well," she said, "I suppose now that Dad's snowstorm is no longer news, I probably won't be seeing as much of you." She handed him the top of a dripolator.

"I wouldn't bet on that," David said as he wrapped the dripolator top in his damp dish towel. "What are you doing for breakfast tomorrow?"

"Sunday? Who's kidding whom?" She didn't look up from the suds in the sink. But he could tell she was childishly pleased by his invitation.

"I'm deadly serious," he went on. "If you're game, we can have break-fast at Kelsey's here in town—I guarantee their scrambled eggs, on week-days at least. Then we can take off in what I laughingly call the car. We can always go over Cainfield way and look at the snow country if we need an excuse."

"You mean it?"

"Of course I mean it." She showed him where to put the dripolator top in a hitherto closed cupboard. "How come I haven't met you before?" he asked. "I've been around Westover since I came to Grafton in June."

"Ever been in Briggs' photo shop?" She plunged her hands into the dishwater again.

"Several times."

"Wasn't my fault you didn't meet me, then."

"Dwight said you worked there. Retouching or something."

"You ought to see what I can do for local bridal couples who go pop-eyed when the flash bulb goes off."

"How come? I mean, how come you work there?"

"How come you work at the *Leader?*" She busied herself scrubbing a plate. "It's something to do, I guess."

"You draw or paint or something?"

"I can. But I guess I've never really done much of anything since college except stick around with Dad and help him as much as I can without being a scientist too. It was ten years ago Mother died, and he's still an awfully lonely guy."

"I begin to think I was rather unobservant, not spotting you in Briggs' last summer."

"I think you were too. Look, don't you know how to dry silver yet?" He had picked up a single fork and was methodically polishing it with the towel. She took his towel and picked up a fistful of silver with it from the rinsing rack and thrust it at him. "You'd never get done that way, silly." Guiding his hands, she showed him the right way. He was suddenly very much aware of her nearness and the warm quickness of her fingers. Without premeditation, he took her by the shoulders and kissed her.

For a moment afterwards they looked at each other expectantly, as if between them, they had managed to drop the silver and were awaiting the inevitable crash as it struck the floor and scattered. Then Karen turned away, something about the set of her shoulders guarding against what had happened. "Wonder what they're talking about in the living-room," she said.

"Snow would be my guess," he said, absent-mindedly dropping the dried silver back into the rinsing rack.

"Did snow over in Cainfield, didn't it." She took the towel from him and began to wipe her hands on it without looking at him. "You dried that once," she said, nodding at the rack.

"I guess I did," he said. This time he kissed her in earnest. When she got her hands untangled from the towel, they went from the back of his neck up into his bristly, undisciplined hair. She felt very small in his arms, and very like a lot of things he had missed for a long time, or maybe never had.

At Kelsey's the next morning Karen was there before he was, reading a copy of the *New York Sunday Mirror* over coffee. She wore navy-blue ski-pants with ski-boots, red-banded socks and a plaid shirt. He was glad she had dressed for outdoors, because he had too, and the sun was bright in a clear autumn sky.

"Can't start Sunday off without 'Li'l Abner,' " she explained as he took the stool next to her. "Dad gets the *Boston Herald*, so I read Pogo at home."

"I'm glad you read Pogo," he said. "I had a good time last night."

"So did I." After they had ordered scrambled eggs and orange juice, she folded her arms over her funnypapers and looked at him happily. "What are we going to do today?"

"I don't know. Just drive somewhere. Climb a mountain, maybe. Know any good mountains?"

"Let's stop on the way and see how my snowball is."

He looked at her. "Snowball? What snowball?"

"The one the little boy said got bigger all by itself. You've forgotten already? After all, you took a picture of it."

"So I did. That gives me an idea." He got up and went to the drug-store's newsrack, bringing back a copy of one of the Boston tabloids. His picture of Robin Gort and the snowball was on page three, with a narrative caption about the early snow in Cainfield.

"David, how wonderful!" she exclaimed.

"Forgot for a moment we'd sent it in to the wire service. Didn't think they'd use it." He felt childishly pleased.

"Now we *have* to go see our snowball," she said.

"I've even got my camera in the car in case it's really got bigger," he added.

David felt happier than he had for a long time as they started out. It was still cold, almost freezing. But the sun was bright and warm where its direct rays struck. The New Hampshire hills were deep purple beyond the roads to be travelled. Sunday with Karen. There was something that sounded very right about that—as if his Sundays had always been with Karen. Even his ancient Chevrolet seemed to assume a certain dignity as she climbed into it beside him. He realized with a slight, pleasurable qualm that his life was no longer as entirely his own as it had been before last night.

This time, as they approached Cainfield, the skies continued to be clear—at least there was blue sky showing between dry-looking grey clouds. The roads were clear too. The snow had retreated to the fields where it lay still thickly white. It seemed like an intruder now, with so much green showing still in the fields and woods.

At the crossroads, David turned up the old dirt road that led to the Gorts' house, whistling softly as he guided the car through the softening ruts.

"Dave!" Karen sat up suddenly. "Our snowball's gone, and look who's there!"

A dark blue police Ford had pulled up onto the Gorts' lawn on the other side of the old apple tree. Down the slope near the henhouse stood a small group of people. In the group David recognized Robin Gort and his mother. Also in the group was a uniformed policeman and Cainfield's police Chief, Osbert L. Carmichael.

6 . . .

CARMICHAEL, RUDDY-FACED as ever, and wearing a civilian leather jacket, had a broad grin and a "good-morning" for David and Karen as they joined the group. But otherwise he seemed to take their presence for granted and offered no explanation of what was going on. He was talking to Mrs. Gort, who seemed on the verge of hysterics. An unshaven man, with woolen underwear showing through the open collar of his checkered shirt, who seemed to be Mr. Gort, stood grim-faced just behind her, holding Robin's hand. The uniformed policeman stood a few steps below the group, peering through the window of the henhouse, apparently watching someone inside.

"Now, Mrs. Gort," Carmichael was saying, "if you'll just tell us calm as possible exactly what happened, could be we could help some. Can't exactly bring back your chickens for you. Could start getting an idea who or what did it, though."

"Well," she began breathlessly, "my husband and the boy here and I was over to my cousin Rachel's in Grantham all evening. Kind of late when we got back, it was—late for us, that is. We're not folks to stay up nights much. Got back about ten thirty and seemed like everything was all right. Snow had stopped, and Bert was kind of tired. Guess he didn't bother to check the hens, or anything like that—though, mind you, he usually does.

"Well, we all went to bed and didn't hear a thing. Nothing out of the ordinary, that is. Bailey's dog barked some next door. But if anything had been after the hens here, they'd have made a racket, and I guess

[34]

we'd have heard. Guess Bert can tell you the rest better than I can. . . ." She turned to the man behind her.

Bert cleared his throat. "First I knowd something was wrong," he said, "was when I went to feed the hens before breakfast. There they was, stiff on the floor, every last one of 'em. Wasn't no blood or feathers around as if somethin' had been after 'em. Figured they must have frozen to death—but don't see how they could have, only as cold as it got last night. Little snow on the floor, must have blown in through the cracks. But not near enough to suffocate 'em."

"No marks on them at all?" Carmichael asked.

"Well, you saw 'em," Bert said almost belligerently. "Weren't torn apart none. But you saw how they was all kind of dried-up looking. Seemed like mice had been chewing at their legs too."

Carmichael shook his head. "Didn't look like anyone could have got into the henhouse. Door was latched. No windows broken open. No holes big enough for anything to have got in under the walls. You have any trouble like this before with your stock?" Gort shook his head slowly. "Want to take a look?" Carmichael seemed to notice the presence of David and Karen for the first time. "Damndest thing I ever saw."

"Not sure I do," Karen said. But she followed David and the others down to the henhouse. She saw that Robin was walking beside her. His hands, without gloves, still had bandages on the palms. "How are your hands?" she asked him.

"All right, I guess. Still sore."

"What about your snowball? What happened to that?"

"Rolled down the hill, I guess. You can see where it fetched up against the henhouse." She noticed a few lumps of snow, still lying where he pointed.

"Did it get any bigger after all?" she asked.

"Must have, else it would have stayed put."

As they entered the henhouse, Carmichael introduced David to a tall, thin man in a grey suit who was bending over the inert form of one of the chickens. The man was Dr. Callan, head of the small animals division of Cainfield's veterinary hospital. He nodded briefly and stood up.

Karen clung involuntarily to David as she looked at the interior of the henhouse. The remains of the eighteen hens were clustered at the far end, some of them with their wings and feet outspread as if they had struggled in dying. David bent down over the nearest of the still forms. Under the scarcely disturbed feathers, the skin was withered, and the closed eyes seemed to have sunk almost to the bottoms of their sockets. The grey, scaly covering of the feet had been mostly eaten away, revealing white bone. But there was no blood anywhere, and almost no loose feathers.

"I've never seen anything like it," Dr. Callan admitted. "Almost complete dehydration." David noticed there was a peculiar odor in the henhouse—a little like wet mould.

"Any way to account for it?" Carmichael asked Dr. Callan.

"In all my experience . . ." the veterinary began. "I'm afraid I'd hesitate to give any kind of an opinion without a detailed microscopic and bacteriological examination."

"You don't think any kind of animal could have got them?" David asked. "A weasel or something that might have sucked their blood?"

"Not a chance," Callan said. "Even if a weasel had got in here, he wouldn't have killed more than one or two at most. And they wouldn't have looked like this afterwards. No, that's definitely out. It wasn't any animal that did this."

"What was it, then?" Karen asked in a small voice.

"Wish I knew." The doctor shook his head and looked down at the remains of the hens. Then he turned to the Gorts. "You people have your stock insured?"

Gort nodded.

"I can sign anything you need with the insurance company. I don't think it was your fault. But in the meantime I wouldn't say anything more about this than you can help to anybody. I'll need to take a couple of the chickens down to the hospital for examination. But I'd rather not have any rumors starting until we know whether we have a new poultry disease on our hands or not."

"Guess that'll have to go for you too," Carmichael told David. "Nothing for publication until we give you the word."

"Of course," David said as they left the henhouse. Carmichael turned to the Gorts. "Mighty sorry about this," he said, "but I'm afraid there isn't much more we can do for you. Have to leave it up to Dr. Callan from here. I'll have Jim here," he nodded towards the uniformed officer, "check—who is it, the Edgertons across the street, and I'll look in on Bailey down the road just in case he heard anything. And Bailey's got some chickens, I think. Like to see if they're OK. But if nothing more turns up, I guess that's about it as far as the police are concerned."

"Mind if we go with you?" David asked as Carmichael headed for his car. Carmichael hesitated, his ruddy face unusually serious. David could see he was deeply troubled about the Gorts' chickens. Carmichael wasn't very bright, David had decided when he first met him. But he knew almost everybody in Cainfield, and had a warm personal interest in helping them with their problems—at least any problems he was trained to handle. The kind of problems Cainfield had that called for the police were usually simple. Carmichael wasn't equipped to handle anything that wasn't.

"That's the real McCoy about nothing for publication, you know," he said. "Long as you understand that, glad to have you along." He brightened when David introduced Karen more fully. "I've met the professor," he said. "He's got a laboratory up in the woods around here somewhere, hasn't he? Maybe we ought to call him in to help us on this."

"He'd be glad to do anything he could," Karen said. They got into the police car and swung down the road towards Bailey's farm. "How do you figure it, Dave?" Carmichael asked.

"Guess I'm as much in the dark as you," David said.

"Lots of people around here have chickens," Carmichael went on. "Going to be hell to pay if we have an epidemic. Kind of scary, wasn't it, the way they was all shrivelled up?"

"Please, let's not talk about it," Karen urged.

There was no sign of life as they pulled into Bailey's yard. "Probably isn't home," Carmichael said. "We can take a look at his chickens, anyway, though, and see if they're alive and kicking."

"Must be home," David said. "The door's open."

"Light's on in the kitchen too." Karen peered through the open door. They knocked, but there was no answer. When repeated knocking brought nothing but a silence that seemed almost oppressive, they went around back through snow that still lay an inch or two deep in the dooryard. Bailey's Model A Ford was still parked out back, and the chickens all seemed healthy and undisturbed. But there was no sign of Bailey or his collie who, Carmichael said, always barked and made a great commotion over visitors.

"Seem to be tracks going out into the field," David said, "maybe he's . . . There's something out there too." About a hundred yards out in the field something dark was lying in the snow. And suddenly David didn't like the looks of what he saw. "Wait here, Karen!" he said, and started running towards the object in the snow. When he reached it, he stared down at it a moment in stark disbelief. Then a gust of nausea swept over him. "Chief! Come here, quick!" he managed in a hoarse voice. But, sensing his urgency, Carmichael had followed him as he ran out and reached his side a moment later.

"Holy mother of God!" he whispered. Then David remembered Karen. She had started after them. He ran back to her and grabbed her shoulders.

"Karen! Don't go out there!"

"David! What is it?" Her eyes began to reflect some of the horror in his.

"It's Bailey, Karen. He's . . . He's dead."

7 . . .

"DEAD?"

Karen caught David's arms and looked up at him, her eyes very wide. "David, what happened? Did somebody kill him?" She looked out towards Carmichael, who was walking briskly back from the dark object in the snow.

"I don't know, Karen. Something awful's happened. I . . ." Just then Carmichael came up to them, very red-faced and out of breath.

"This is something for the sheriff and Doc Markel," he managed between puffs as he headed for the car. He stopped and looked at David. "You beat it up to Edgerton's," he said, "and tell Parker to get the hell down here as fast as he can!"

Karen half walked, half ran through the snow to keep up with David as they hurried up the hill. "David . . . what happened . . . tell me . . . !" she gasped as she did her best to keep up with him.

"Don't ask questions, darling. Not now." But he stopped a moment, waiting for her, and took her hand for reassurance.

Parker, the uniformed officer, had just crossed the road from the Edgertons' to the Gorts' holding a leather boot in his hand. He grinned as he saw them, holding up the boot apologetically. "Might be a clue," he explained. "Mrs. Edgerton said mice chewed it on her porch this morning." But his beardless face, which David thought looked very young under the blue policeman's cap, clouded and grew serious as he saw the look in David's eyes.

David glanced at the Gorts who, some paces away, were still standing by the door of their henhouse, watching whatever Dr. Callan was doing inside. Then, in a low voice, he explained to Parker what had happened. "Guess it's best not to let the Gorts know what's up," he suggested.

"Guess you're right," said Parker, whose lips had pursed into a silent whistle at the news. The Gorts scarcely looked up as the three of them walked past, trying to avoid any appearance of haste.

Carmichael was standing by the car when they returned. The intermittent piping of its radio, indicating that the Cainfield station was broadcasting on another frequency, was faintly audible. "Sheriff McEwen's on his way," he said. "Doc Markel'll be here any minute." Then he turned to David and Karen. "Dave, you'd better get Miss—Miss Cruickshank away from here. I don't think she'll want to see what's out there."

Karen swallowed hard and clung to David's hand. "I can take it," she said. She looked at David. "Maybe . . . maybe I'd better be in on it too," she added.

Carmichael shrugged. "You're press," he told David. "She'll have to be your responsibility, though." Together the four of them advanced again through the snow toward the dark thing that lay in the field, looking from a distance like a piece of windblown paper sacking. As they approached Karen clung harder and harder to David's hand. As they reached the spot, she gave an involuntary cry and buried her face in the shoulder of his field jacket.

John Bailey lay on his back in the snow, his knees drawn up a little, a fine powder of snow still clinging to his windbreaker, corduroy pants and heavily booted feet. He lay on his back with his arms outflung. The overturned lantern lay a foot or two from his mittened left hand. The stock of his rifle protruded from the snow near his right. There was nothing to indicate he had met a strange or violent death except his face, staring nakedly up at the sky from under a visored cap. This was what had made Karen cry out.

Bailey's face was brownish grey and withered like the face of a mummy. The shrivelled lips were drawn back from the teeth in a fixed, hideous grimace. White bone showed where taut skin had withered away at the bridge of the nose. Worst of all were the eyes. The dried-up lids had sunk deep into what had apparently become almost empty sockets.

Not far from Bailey's body, a light sprinkling of snow covered the remains of a very emaciated-looking collie dog.

For a moment all four stood transfixed without speaking, all except

Karen unable to take their eyes from what they saw. Only Karen kept her face buried in David's shoulder. Then, by unspoken mutual consent, they turned and moved a few paces away. Karen, holding her head up now, was very white. So was Parker, whose Adam's apple worked conspicuously above his uniform collar. Carmichael's face had turned from red to mottled purple. David felt a haunting sense of uneasiness—as if neither the thing in the snow that had been Bailey, nor they themselves who had stood looking at it, could have any reality—it was too fantastic.

"That's the Goddamndest thing I've ever seen," Carmichael said finally in a strained voice. For a moment he seemed to have completely forgotten his official capacity. Then he looked at Parker and collected himself with a visible jerk. "What the Goddam hell are you carrying that old boot around for?" he wanted to know.

Parker seemed relieved at the sound of his Chief's anger, and some color came back into his face. His Adam's apple stopped working. "Mrs. Edgerton said it got chewed up by something on her porch this morning," he said simply. "Guess I should have . . ." He trailed off, not knowing exactly what he should have done.

"So it got chewed by something. OK, hang onto it." But Carmichael wasn't thinking about the boot. He was staring towards the road beyond Bailey's house, as if, David thought, he were conscious of not being able to think of anything to do until he heard the siren indicating the arrival of Dr. Markel and the ambulance, or the police car with the official photographer.

"Let me see that," David said suddenly, and took the boot from Parker. He had remembered what Dr. Callan had said about the legs of the chickens in the henhouse. "As if they were chewed by mice," he remembered. Then he thought of what was lying behind him in the snow and tossed the boot away in a sudden fit of revulsion. He forced his thoughts back to reality. Karen was standing beside him, frightened to death, and she needed his calmness.

Parker automatically retrieved the boot, as if there hadn't been anything funny about his throwing it away, and started dusting the snow off of it.

With a coolness befitting the job which required him, as Cainfield's medical referee, occasionally to pronounce a hunting accident or suicide victim dead, in addition to his regular practice, Dr. Markel examined the remains of Bailey swiftly, efficiently and without visible indication of distaste other than a preliminary whistle of astonishment.

"He's dead," he announced finally as he stood up, while two ambulance attendants from the Cainfield hospital stood by ready with a stretcher. "Been dead about twelve hours, well as I could guess." His voice was calm. But David noticed how strained and masklike his face had become. The doctor looked toward David and Karen. "As to the condition of the face . . . cause of death for that matter . . . can't say a thing till I get him somewhere else." He glanced dubiously at Carmichael. "You'll be getting a picture, I suppose."

Carmichael thrust out his lower lip. "Routine. Have to. But, hell, nobody killed him, did they?"

"Something killed him. But I think we'd better get him out of here fast and as quietly as possible, soon as you get your picture." He was still looking at David and Karen. Carmichael belatedly performed introductions, explaining to the doctor who they were. Dr. Markel nodded and took the Chief aside for a moment. When Carmichael came back, he looked grave.

"Dave," he said, "there's nothing for the press about this except maybe Bailey had a heart attack if you gotta use it. We oughta know better by the time you go to press. Play ball with us and don't say anything about it in the meantime and we'll let you and Miss Cruickshank stick around since you were in on it. But you better play ball with us. This looks serious. That's all any of the dailies are going to get—least till the doc here gets a chance to do his stuff."

Just then two cars pulled into the Bailey driveway, one behind the other. A moment later Dr. Callan, who had come to check out with Carmichael about the chickens, and Sheriff McEwen, who had come in a police car with Art Lacey, a Cainfield photographer who did official police work on the side, joined the group.

Sheriff McEwen, who, according to New Hampshire law, served as the legal arm of the state throughout the county in all matters too large for local police to handle alone or not specifically requiring state police intervention, was a large, good-natured man, who didn't look like anybody's idea of a sheriff and enjoyed being kidded about it. David remembered hearing about the joke his office employes had recently played on him when they tacked a "wanted" poster on the bulletin board with his photograph and name heading a list of minor fleshly indulgences.

But McEwen wasn't smiling as he stood beside the photographer, looking down at what was left of Bailey. His normally cherubic countenance had assumed the color of putty. "Jesus . . . !" He sucked hard on a cigarette that had gone out while he listened to as much as anybody knew.

The photographer, a tall, angular man with an expressionless face, snapped his camera at various angles and nodded to the others, and the stretcher men went about their task. Dr. Callan seemed more impressed with the remains of the collie dog than with what had happened to Bailey. He bent down and examined the stiff form in the snow for a moment as Carmichael quietly instructed Parker to go back to the entrance of the driveway and make sure the Gorts didn't drift down to see what was going on.

Callan rose slowly, almost painfully from his examination of the dog and glanced again at Bailey, who by now was on a stretcher. Then he ran a hand through his thinning hair and looked at Dr. Markel.

"You better take a look at the Gorts' chickens up the road, Orin," he said. "My guess is Bailey's dog died of the same thing." He looked up at the group suddenly and defiantly. "If my opinion's any good, so did Bailey!"

8 . . .

To David, McEwen didn't look like a man of action. But he apparently was when necessary. Carmichael seemed to have learned to rely on his decision when possible in matters that overextended his own horizon. As McEwen went over the ground and asked questions about what had happened, an outsider would have thought sheriff and local police were, in this case, a team working in perfect harmony, rather than a pair of very puzzled officials, the more completely puzzled of the two gratefully following the lead of the one who at least appeared less so.

After Carmichael's introduction and brief explanation that Karen and David were there because they happened to be in on the discovery of the body, and understood nothing was to be released for the press as yet, the sheriff nodded at the two and seemed to accept their presence without further comment.

When the ambulance was gone with what was left of Bailey in back and Art Lacey fussing with his photographic plates alongside the driver in the front seat, McEwen stood at the spot where the body had lain, scowling down at the remains of the collie dog. "Looks like it could have been done by some kind of acid," he said half to himself, "except it doesn't seem to have hurt the fur any." He turned to Dr. Callan. "You say the chickens up there looked like this too?"

"That's right," the veterinary said. "Looked like extensive dehydration. Not much damage to the feathers, though."

McEwen turned to Dr. Markel. "What about Bailey? Same thing, you think?"

Dr. Markel scratched his chin. "Of course I haven't seen the chickens," he began cautiously, "but I would say there was very marked evidence of dehydration of skin-tissues in both Bailey and the dog here. Impossible from here to say whether it was the cause of death, or happened afterwards."

"What might have caused it, do you think?"

Markel shook his head. "Can't say about what caused either the death or the dehydration till I get through with him in the lab."

"Any idea what *could* cause something like that . . . Bailey's face, I mean, and . . ."

"Lots of things could, I guess. Strong acid. More likely a strong alkali —something like quicklime with a strong affinity for moisture. But that just doesn't seem to make sense in this case. It would have affected Bailey's clothes and the dog's hair. And if you've got any ideas about how a man and a dog could get quicklime all over them out here in the middle of a field . . . !"

"No trace of any chemical around the henhouse up there either," Callan agreed, "and no indication anyone could have got in."

"Why would anyone want to do a thing like that anyway?" Carmichael wondered out loud.

"Whether they'd have reason to or not," McEwen said, "what I'd like to know is how the hell anybody could have?" He turned to Markel again. "Any chance it could be some kind of disease, Doc?"

"If so, I've never heard of anything like it—not that could produce an effect like that overnight anyway."

"You, Doc?" McEwen looked at Callan.

Callan shook his head. "God, no! Wouldn't want to take a chance on saying for sure it wasn't though, till I have a chance to make tests. But now that I've seen this . . ." he nodded towards the snow at McEwen's feet ". . . I'd say no. I don't think it could be anything pathological." He looked at Markel.

"Unless we've got something entirely new and pretty horrible on our hands," Markel said. "But I'll go along with Callan. If it's pathological it's beyond my experience too." He glanced from Carmichael to McEwen. "You two going to need me any more here? I'll try and have a report for you by this evening."

"Just one more thing, Doc," McEwen said. "You say Bailey had been dead about twelve hours?"

"Near as I could tell. Hour or two either way. Ought to be able to place it between nine and midnight yesterday evening."

When the doctor had driven off, McEwen turned to Callan. "What are you doing about the chickens?" he asked.

"I've got my assistant up at the henhouse," Callan said. "Think we'd better dispose of the hens, except for what we need in the lab, right away just in case. We'll take care of the dog too. I've told the Gorts they better keep quiet about the hens if they don't want any complications with the insurance. Said they could say I'm investigating what killed 'em, but not to go into any details."

"You don't imagine they'll keep quiet, do you?" McEwen smiled grimly.

"Not with Ada Edgerton living across the street," Carmichael put in.

"No," Callan said, "that was just routine. It'll get around all right. But as long as no one connects it up with what happened to Bailey . . ."

"They won't," McEwen said. He looked at David. "You work for Dwight Heron, don't you?" he asked. "Well, you tell him anything you want, 'cause I'll be in touch with him. But don't tell anyone else. We'll have a regular obituary for you on Bailey. After all, a heart attack at his age isn't too surprising. But you just forget anything else you've seen around here today, and I promise you you'll get the whole story when and if the time comes. The dailies aren't going to get anything more than you."

"That's fair enough," David said.

McEwen turned back towards the body of the dog. "The way I figure it," he began, "is Bailey must have heard something—something that must have sounded like an animal or an intruder—otherwise he wouldn't have had his gun and the lantern . . ."

"The Gorts said this morning they heard a dog barking last night," Karen remembered. She was still standing close to David, her arm linked in his, her face very pale.

"That would tie in," Carmichael said. "Must have been the dog barking gave him the idea of investigating."

"And so he goes and investigates, and we find him and the dog like . . ." McEwen turned to the others. "That was no animal did that to Bailey's face—no natural animal!" McEwen's eyes widened for a moment. Then he seemed suddenly embarrassed at what he had said. "Did Bailey have any enemies?" he asked abruptly.

"Didn't even have any relatives, far as I know," Carmichael said.

"Lived all by himself. Don't think anyone would have wanted to hurt him."

David suddenly remembered the boot Parker had clung to. "This probably is beside the point and also fantastic," he began. He picked up the boot, which Parker had finally left in the snow when he went to guard the entrance to the driveway, and explained how it had been found on the Edgertons' snowy side porch that morning, just across the road from the Gorts'. McEwen and Carmichael studied the place where the upper had been eaten away from the sole with some interest. "What's the connection?" McEwen asked finally.

"This boot was apparently standing out in the snow," David explained. "There was snow in the Gorts' henhouse, and Bailey and the dog here were found in the snow. I know this sounds pretty far-fetched. But you know how smog can sometimes be poisoned with a chemical that can hurt or even kill people. Well, something's happened to this boot that could be like what happened to Bailey and the chickens. Do you suppose some chemical or something could have got into the snow in this particular area that . . ."

"Yes," Karen said suddenly, "and what about the Gort boy who hurt his hands playing in the snow."

McEwen looked at David with a combination of new respect and resentment. "Nice piece of deduction, son. Could be the most sensible idea we've come up with yet. Coupla things wrong with it, though.

"First place there isn't any way the snow around here could get polluted. Nearest factory chimneys are in Lebanon and Claremont. And nothing comes out of them that could hurt anybody much 'less they stuck their nose over the top of the chimney. Second place we've all been standing here in the snow where Bailey died for quite a spell now. Nothing wrong with my boots. How about yours?" Each of them looked at his boots and found no sign of the peculiar fraying. Finally McEwen pulled off a glove and scooped up a handful of snow in his bare hand. He held it towards the others for a few moments as it melted slowly in his bare palm. Then he brushed the snow off, flexed his fingers and put his glove back on.

"Nice try, son," he said. "Almost wish you'd been right. Then at least we'd have something to go on. Course I don't know yet whether my hand will drop off an hour from now. But if I'd been Bailey, I'd have had plenty of chance to get back to my warm kitchen." He offered the boot to Carmichael. "Guess we can give this back to the owner," he said. But Carmichael was down on one knee near where the outline of Bailey's body was still visible in the snow.

"This may be something, Ed," he told McEwen over his shoulder. The others gathered closer.

"Ground's fairly well chewed up where we've been walking," Carmichael said, "but not so's you can't notice something kind of funny—ain't any footprints leading up to either Bailey or the dog."

"Well, it did snow yesterday," Karen suggested.

"Not that late," Carmichael said. "Stopped snowing something after four yesterday. Doc Markel says Bailey didn't die until about nine at the earliest. Besides, you can see both Bailey's tracks and the dog's quite plain up to about five yards from here."

It was true. Across the field the old man's tracks, and those of his dog were still as clear as the tracks David, Karen and the police had made themselves. Then just short of where the body had been found, they faded to indistinct impressions and then vanished entirely as if they had been wiped away.

"Wasn't enough wind to cause any drifting," Carmichael added, "not anywhere else around anyway. And the snow's no deeper here than it is anywhere else."

"How do you account for that?" David asked McEwen.

"God only knows!" The sheriff threw away his cigarette with a violent gesture. "But don't you forget what I told you about what you've seen here this morning as far as the paper's concerned. There isn't going to be any panic around here as long as I'm sheriff!" Then suddenly he sighed and thrust his hands deep in the pockets of his trenchcoat.

"And don't think there couldn't be—Jesus God!"

9 . . .

McEwen told David he wouldn't give him anything on the results of the Bailey autopsy by phone. But if he wanted to drop around at the Cainfield police station about five in the evening, he and Carmichael would be available, and might at least have something from Markel and Callan. In the meantime, anybody who had to know, would be told Bailey died of a heart attack, and that the fate of the Gorts' chickens was being investigated.

"Might be best if you let Heron be for the moment, seeing it's Sunday," McEwen added. "But if you have to call him, don't say anything on the Goddam phone and tell him to see me first if he comes over. I'll see him later anyhow." He hesitated a moment. "Don't think any of the other papers know anything yet—otherwise they'd have been around. But they damned sure won't find out anything if they do show up!"

Karen maintained her equilibrium until she got back into David's car beside him. Then she crumpled, burying her face against him and shivering. "Oh, Dave, it's too awful! It can't be true!" He pressed his hand into her pale brown hair, holding her head where it was.

"You shouldn't have been there," he said. "It was my fault. Try not to think about it." He stroked her hair automatically, searching, against the cold uneasiness he felt in his own heart, for some kind of reassurance he could give her. Except for the stroking pressure of his hand, he found none.

"David . . ." Her head tensed under his hand. "Something terrible did happen, didn't it?"

"Well, yes—of course it was terrible. Anything like that is terrible."

She pulled her head away from him and sat up. "I mean something really terrible . . . Something that frightened the sheriff and all of them."

"Well, it frightened you, very understandably. You shouldn't have seen what you saw."

"All right. So I shouldn't have seen what I saw! But I did see it. Can you explain it?"

"There is an explanation. There has to be." His hands were cold, and there was a gnawing feeling under his ribs, like the feeling you sometimes have when you drink too much coffee in the morning without bothering to include breakfast with it. This time it wasn't lack of breakfast. What they had seen had shaken him too, made everything seem unreal—everything except Karen, that is. And he felt strangely guilty about her—as if he were wrong just to be sitting there in the car with her after everything that had happened.

"Karen, I'm sorry," he said.

"Sorry? Why should you be sorry?"

"Sort of spoiled our Sunday."

"Sort of spoiled Mr. Bailey's, too."

"I didn't mean that to sound as selfish as it did."

"I know." She sat beside him, staring straight ahead of her. He looked at her profile, angry at what had happened. He wasn't angry now so much because it had been horrible, particularly for her, but indeed selfishly because it had changed this particular Sunday.

People were never really as concerned about death, even violent death, he realized, as they went through the motions of being—unless of course it happened to somebody they knew or loved. He noticed how the light caught on the pale down of her cheeks.

After a moment he turned her face towards him with the tips of his fingers and kissed her. She started up in a moment of instinctive resistance, then leaned against the back of the seat, tensely compliant. Through parka and woolen shirt, her body, like a bird's under thick feathers, felt surprisingly warm and small in his arms.

"This is a hell of a time for this sort of thing," he said after a few moments, his face close enough to hers so he felt the small current of her suddenly expelled breath.

"Must there be a right time and a wrong time?" She lay back against the seat, looking at him. "You called me 'darling' a while ago, coming up the hill. Did you mean it?"

[50]

"If I said it, I must have meant it." He pushed a stray wisp of hair away from her forehead.

"I'm glad I was with you when this happened," she said.

"I'm glad you were. But under the circumstances, I think we'd better get the hell out of the Gorts' front yard."

"I think we also better notice that it's snowing again," she said.

Since the discovery of Bailey's body, neither had noticed how the soot-grey clouds had again blotted out the sun. And now small dry flakes were falling again. Where they sat in the parked car in front of the Gorts' farmhouse, they were falling sparsely still. But to the north Barker Mountain was already almost invisible behind a thick grey pall that could only be heavy snow.

Karen looked at him, no trace of the mood of a moment ago left in her eyes. "Oh, David, do you suppose Dad was right about the snow after all—on top of what's happened . . . ?"

"Is he at home now, Karen?"

"No, he'll be at the lab now."

"Do you know how to get there?" She nodded.

"I have a feeling we better get the hell up there as fast as we can," he said. He shifted the car into gear with an unnecessary roar, turned it around, and gunned it back onto the dirt road in the direction they had come. "Turn right at Westover corner," was all she said.

In the few moments it had taken them to get under way the falling snow had thickened. It seemed to swirl up at them from the road in a hurried, blinding mass. Frowning with concentration, he leaned closer to the windshield, as if it would help him to see the road ahead.

"David . . ." she began finally. "Do you think what happened could have had something to do with the snow?"

"You heard the sheriff," he said without taking his eyes from the windshield. "Besides, I remember you were making snowballs with your bare hands while I was taking pictures in front of the Gorts'. Didn't seem to hurt you any more than it hurt the sheriff just now when he spoiled my theory." She looked at her palms automatically and said nothing. "But it oughtn't to be snowing like this," he added, "not after the way it has already."

David slowed down a moment later as he came up to a car, headed in the same direction, which was parked along the side of the road, the owner, dimly visible through the flying flakes, leaning over the open radiator hood. Karen cranked down the window on her side and called out, "Need any help?" They both recognized the microtus man they had met the day before in the hotel.

The microtus man recognized them immediately, smiling appreciatively as they stopped and got out. "Awfully glad you came along," he said. "Battery's down and I guess I need a push. Ever seen anything like this for this time of year?"

"What brings you up here, Manning?" David asked as he looked at the battered-looking ten-year-old Plymouth parked at a slant in the steep ditch of the road. "Still looking for field mice?"

"Yes, and you ought to see what I found!" Manning's eyes kindled with enthusiasm. For a moment he had forgotten the stalled car. "Have you got a minute?"

"Not much of a minute," David said. "We'd better start pushing you if we're going to."

"I really wish you'd take a look at what I found first," Manning said. "It's extraordinary—really quite extraordinary." Before David could protest he had taken a brown canvas satchel out of the back seat and opened the zipper top. He removed a wad of Kleenex tissue and began to open it up. "I found three of them right along the other side of the road there where the bark was all gnawed off some chokecherry bushes. Really extraordinary."

David watched him patiently as he unfolded the Kleenex. The tissue contained the body of a dead field mouse. "It hasn't been dead long," Manning explained. "Rigor mortis has scarcely begun yet. But look how it's withered, and the tail—nothing left but bone . . ."

David and Karen peered at the small lifeless object. David felt a tingling of horror along the back of his neck.

"You say you have more like this?" he asked.

"Three of them, yes."

"Where did you find them?"

"I told you, in the snow, right across the road there."

"How long ago?"

"Just now. Twenty minutes ago."

"Do you—have you any idea what did this to them?"

"No, frankly, I don't. I've never seen anything like it before. That's why I wanted to show them to you . . ."

David bit his lip in momentary indecision. "Look," he said finally, "I know it sounds funny, but will you let us have one of them . . . ?"

"Well, I . . . I had planned on taking them back to . . ."

"Just one. It's very important."

Manning looked at him strangely. "You . . . you know something about this?"

"I may before long," David said.

"But I really don't think I . . ."

"Look, if you want to get pushed out of the ditch, just give me one of those mice and don't ask questions. You staying at the Waverton?" Beginning to look completely bewildered, Manning nodded. He surrendered the mouse to David.

"But . . . I still don't understand."

"You will. We'll be in touch with you there. Now get in and put it in gear." When they had got Manning started and watched his car disappear through the snow ahead, David thrust the mouse wrapped in Kleenex more securely into the side pocket of his field jacket.

"This gets worse and worse, Karen," he said.

"Is it the same thing, Dave—same as Bailey and the chickens?" He nodded.

"You sure your father will be there—at the lab, I mean?"

"Yes. You're going to show him the mouse?"

"What can we lose? He might be able to help." He shifted gears and the car lurched down the dirt road through the snow. "I can't help feeling there's a connection between this thing and the snow somewhere."

"Dave, you don't think Dad . . . ?"

"Karen, we don't know anything about this. Neither do the police. He might be able to help us. There's something wrong about all this snow too. Something's happening. I don't say your father had anything to do with it. That was really just a gag to start with. But who could help us better than he could? Will he mind our coming?"

"Probably. He keeps his lab pretty secret. About as secret as you can keep anything around here. Most people don't even know he has this place, let alone where it is."

"You're worried about your father, aren't you?" he said. "About what he'll think about the snow, and the mice and Bailey on top of it?" She remained silent. For a while they both listened to the click of the windshield wiper. Beyond the windshield wiper was a sea of spinning whiteness now, hurtling against the speed of the car. Now and then the whiteness of the road ahead and the shadows of whitened trees, their leaves still incongruously green, were distinct for a few moments, but only between gusts of wind that blotted everything out.

"Maybe I have reason to be worried," Karen said. "Not about the snow and things, but about Dad. He isn't well, Dave. His fears are all in his own mind. If I thought there was any way of keeping him from hearing what has happened, I'd say we shouldn't go here tonight. But he will hear. So I guess it's better he hears from us first."

"What about the experiments?"

"They're important to him, Dave. He's lonely since Mother died, and they're all he has to do. I don't know whether he's really doing anything or not. What he told me about it doesn't make much sense. What he told you and Dwight yesterday evening about the snow in Cainfield going on indefinitely was all nonsense. But it made him feel important."

David was silent a moment. "So maybe we shouldn't show him the mouse and tell him what has happened. If what you say is true, he'll be worried enough because it's snowing again."

"No, David. That's exactly what we should tell him—what has happened. If we can get him interested in your mouse, it may bring him back to reality a bit. Don't mistake me, Dave, he isn't off the beam or anything like that. But when he isn't teaching at Grafton during the week, he gets so absorbed in these researches of his out here at the lab that he just isn't around as far as anything else is concerned."

"Wouldn't it be a good idea to persuade him to give up the lab, then?"

"Yes, it would be a wonderful idea. But how can I? It's all he lives for. It's funny," she went on, "when you decided we had to come out and see him just now—after it started snowing again—it was for a very different reason. You thought he might be responsible for the snow—what else could you think after what he said himself last night? But if we can get him interested in the mouse, and in everything that's been happening today, it will really be very good for him."

David was silent, straining his eyes through the windshield to see where he was going. The old car moaned and skittered as it fought its way over the rough road that was already white with the new snow.

"I hope you're right," he said. He reached over and squeezed Karen's hand. She didn't respond to his touch. She was staring straight ahead through the clouded windshield, and even touching her hand, he felt no communication with her.

The empty feeling inside him came back along with a sudden conviction that she hadn't been telling the truth about her father.

10 . . .

THIS IS GOING to be a real blizzard, David thought.

He had never thought about snow much in the years he had lived in New York. Snow in New York City was seldom more than a soggy fluff that settled like a wet skin on the streets, giving them an illusion of pristine cleanliness for a few hours until it got melted or shovelled away, or trampled into muddy grime. After a while it became nothing more than a refuse of brown slush in the gutters that didn't have much effect on the comings and goings of mankind.

But this was different. He listened now with growing respect to the wail of the wind that hurled small, hard flakes against the windshield. He noticed the needles of cold air that reached through the partly open panel of the front window. This time it isn't any fluke storm, he thought. This time it is really going to be something.

"Warm enough?" he asked Karen, who huddled in silence beside him.

"Only just," she said. The car heater was making a growling noise, but hadn't produced much heat as yet. He was not even sure it was capable of doing so. He had bought the car in the spring and, until now, had never had occasion to try the heater.

The road was winding blacktop for a couple of miles beyond the Westover corner, and still covered only with a shifting film of snow. It was not yet slippery in most places. What made driving difficult was that it was seldom possible to see more than twenty feet ahead through the flying flakes. Finally Karen indicated a turn to the right.

"Good Lord," David exclaimed as he swung the car into the turnoff.

The road was a narrow dirt one, already solid white with no wheel-ruts. And the steep bulk of Barker Mountain had risen continuously on their right for the past two miles. "You mean we've got to go up the mountain in this?"

"Not quite," Karen said. "The road follows a ravine along a little brook up to where Dad's place is. It's not too steep."

It wasn't steep, but it was completely wild. There were no signs of habitation, and a thick forest of birch, red maple and spruce crowded the road on either side as it followed the course of the small, half snow-covered brook. The road was too narrow to pass anyone—too narrow even to attempt to turn around. It was good it wasn't steep, David thought. In the midst of a snow like this, dressed as lightly as they were, it wouldn't be funny to get stuck.

"How did your father happen to find this place?" he asked. He was uncomfortably aware of Karen's silence.

"Dad bought it from an old hermit who used to live here back when I was a kid," Karen said. "The old character trundled happily off to Florida on the proceeds of the sale. It used to be a mill or something. Has good water power from where the stream's damned up behind the place, and Dad had electricity put in and made it into a lab. Put a lot of money into it, I guess. But you wouldn't know it from the outside. Looks like something out of a 'Frankenstein' movie. I guess most people around here don't even know it's still there. Nobody, except maybe a few people on the Grafton faculty, know anything about what Dad's got there. He had out-of-town people install the equipment. He wanted privacy and—well, he's certainly got it."

David swung the car around the last sharp curve and they came to where the road ended in a wide, circular clearing. At the far end of the clearing stood Professor Cruickshank's car, already dusted with snow. Beyond it stood the old mill. Karen's description of it had been quite accurate, David thought.

It was a grey, clapboard structure that looked at least a hundred years old. Set close against the mountain slope, which went up almost vertically behind it, it rose like a wooden parody of a Rhineland castle from one end of a small stone dam, over which the water of the brook still trickled unfrozen. On the side nearest the dam, the building was two stories high, and capped with a small, unkempt-looking gable roof of weathered shingle. The narrowness of this part of the building, with its two small dark windows, gave it the appearance of a tower. The other side of the building was only one story high, and flat-roofed like a shed. There was a larger window on this side, through which a glimmer of light could be seen.

But even this sign of habitation did little to lessen the atmosphere of decrepit gloom that hung about the old building. It occurred to David that the two-story part, with its small windows high up, looked like the head of an old man whose eyes had gone blind with age. Through the falling snow, the building looked spectral and indistinct, like something that only existed in the tired eyes of someone long lost in the forest. Only the car in front of it and the faint light in the first floor window lent reality to its grey silence.

"Nice place to spend the weekend," David commented as they got out of the car, turning up their collars against the snow and biting cold wind.

"Looks grim," Karen agreed, "but he's got it fixed up pretty comfortably—downstairs at least."

The professor had apparently heard the car drive up. He stood in the open front door, waiting silently as they came up. He wore a plaid shirt, open at the collar, with his sleeves rolled up.

"Glad you've come, Karen," he said, "though you shouldn't have in this storm. It was good of Mr. Storm to bring you." He turned to David, his eyes questioning behind their thick glasses.

"Hope you didn't mind David coming too," Karen said, a little breathless from the wind. "But I couldn't very well have got here if he hadn't brought me. And, well—David has something he wants to show you."

"Always glad to see you, Mr. Storm." The professor held out his hand to David with a smile that didn't quite reach his eyes. As he did so, he motioned them inside with his other hand, shut the door after them, and slid the bolt.

The inside of the old mill offered a pleasant contrast to the outside. The room in which they found themselves was painted a cheerful white, and looked like the kitchen of an old New England house. An overhead light was burning because of the darkness of the storm, and at one end of the room a wood fire crackled on a brick hearth. There was a stove, a small icebox, a plain pine table with chairs, and shelves well stocked with kitchen staples. At one end of the room was an army cot, made up with sheets and blankets. Near it stood several packing boxes, apparently full of papers.

"I'm especially glad to see you, Mr. Storm," the professor went on, "because of the fact you are a member of the working press. This time I can tell you in all honesty that I didn't make the weather." His smile this time did reach his eyes.

"Glad of that," David said, unzipping his field jacket. "How do you know you didn't? I mean, how can you be sure this time?"

"Very simple," the professor said. "I have a radio here, and this time the weather reports said it was coming. It also happens to be snowing all over northern New Hampshire—not just Cainfield."

"That doesn't prove you didn't have something to do with the local flurry we had yesterday though, does it?" David asked smiling, as he helped Karen off with her trenchcoat.

"No," the professor said, "and I think I can take the blame for that one rather cheerfully, now that I know it didn't get out of hand. It was really rather foolish of me to be so alarmed about it. But when ordinary, everyday matter—like snow crystals—starts defying the rule books in the laboratory, one can't help being a little cautious. I still have a feeling I'm onto something in that connection, that—well, none of us knows as much as we'd like to." He indicated chairs and suggested some coffee. When Karen volunteered to fix the coffee, he turned back to David.

"Karen says you have something you wanted to show me."

"Get your opinion at least," David said, reaching in his pocket for the crumpled Kleenex with its small burden. "Dead field mouse," he said. "Something funny about it."

"Not exactly in my usual line," the professor said. "Why don't you bring it downstairs to the lab. Like to show you the lab anyhow. Want to come, Karen?" Karen left the coffee heating on the stove and followed them down a steep flight of steps to a basement room that was flooded suddenly with pale mercury-vapor illumination as the professor flipped a switch on the stairs.

The cellar had obviously been completely remodelled. Within its smooth concrete walls was a complete laboratory, with glassed-in shelves of equipment, a linoleum-topped table, with Bunsen burners, apparently supplied by gas cylinders set up in a corner of the room, and what looked like a deep freeze unit. On the linoleum table, and on other tables along the walls, various arrangements of chemical equipment were set up which meant nothing to David. As a scientist, David had never progressed beyond high-school physics.

The professor was pleased with David's comments on the difficulty of getting so much equipment into such an out-of-the-way place, and admitted, smiling rather proudly, that it had taken a number of years and a good deal of money.

At length he took the crumpled tissue from David and unwrapped the remains of the field mouse on the table.

"What exactly did you want my opinion about?" the professor asked. "Looks like an ordinary microtus that's been dead for quite a while." Karen stood back, watching the proceedings with half-concealed aversion as David leaned over the table.

"That's it right there," David said. "I have reason to believe it hasn't been dead more than a few hours."

"But you still must have some reason for bringing it to me," the professor said.

"I don't know whether I have or not." David told him about what had happened. About Bailey and the chickens as well as the mice. When he came to the part about Bailey, the professor sat down on the stool by the table, and his mouth, as he looked up at David, opened for a minute in frank astonishment.

"How could that be so?" he asked.

"Don't know," David said, "but it was."

"And they think it's the same thing as—happened to this mouse?"

"Don't know what *they* think," David told him. "*I* think so. And I've seen both Bailey and the chickens."

"That's ridiculous."

"It happened, Professor Cruickshank, and a man's been killed."

The professor stared down at the mouse for a moment. Then he got up and went to one of the glassed-in cases. He came back with forceps, scalpel and a box of pins. This time both David and Karen leaned over the table.

As they watched, the professor made an expert incision down the mouse's stomach, pinning back the skin as he separated it from the inner membranes. David noticed there were places where the skin, and even the abdominal wall, seemed to be eaten away.

After a few minutes, during which he also examined the mouse's shrivelled tail, feet, and sunken eyes, the professor put down his scalpel and forceps and rose slowly. His face was grey and his hands visibly trembled. "I think I'd better show you something," he said in a toneless voice. "It isn't possible. Yet, I've seen with my own eyes that it is possible."

They followed him as he went to the deep freeze unit and took out a small petri dish. On it was a smudge of brownish powder, with a fragment of some kind of crust in the middle.

"What's that?" David asked.

"It was a piece of bacon rind."

"What happened to it?"

The professor looked at him, his eyes invisible behind the reflection of light on his glasses.

"My snow crystals . . ." he said.

11...

It was silent in the laboratory for a moment, except for a faint hum that came from the gas heating unit, and the occasional murmur of snow-laden wind against the small windows set high in the concrete walls. The professor looked first at his daughter's face, then at David's, seeing the strained question in the eyes of both. Then he put the petri dish he had shown them back in its place in the freezer and turned back to them. There were hard lines of weariness in his face.

"I guess it's time I told you about my crystals," he said. "Up till now there hasn't been any reason to talk about what I was doing—even to you, Karen. You might have guessed my ultimate reasons, my dear; but my methods and experiments couldn't have meant anything to you until—well, until I could come up with some kind of results." He looked at David. "But after what you've told me tonight, Mr. Storm, and after looking at your specimen there, I think I owe you both an explanation. And I hope you both will believe me. I'm not sure that anyone else would—at least not yet."

He was silent a moment, his hands clasped nervously, one over the other, in front of him. Karen sat down on the stool in front of the labora-tory table where the remains of the field mouse were still pinned down. David lifted himself up onto a corner of the table and watched the pro-fessor over his match flame as he lit a cigarette.

"Karen will tell you," the professor went on at length, "that I've been for a long time interested in the structure and nature of crystals—and not," he added, "just as a mineralogist, but as a biochemist." He thrust his hands in his pockets and strode across the floor as if trying to frame the words with which to make a point to a classroom of students.

"One is apt to think of a crystal," he said, "as a cold, lifeless chunk of some mineral or element—something that may be beautiful or ugly from outward view, depending on its composition—but something which, from a layman's point of view, is nothing more than hard cold stone or matter. It doesn't breathe, it doesn't grow, it doesn't change, at least in the span of life we have to observe it. And it has no feelings, or awareness. In short, it's just a piece of rock, or perhaps a grain of the salt with which we season our dinner.

"Often a crystal can be very beautiful. You've both seen quartz or pyrites crystals, or maybe the delicate blue blades of cyanite in mineral collections. But few of us, even the most religious among us, ever think of the wonder behind the making of such crystals.

"We wonder at how our infinitesimal human seed develops so surely into a child and then a man or a woman resembling the father or mother. Talk as you will about mitosis and chromosomes. Beyond a certain point we have to look to something above our comprehension—to a power greater than ourselves, for the answer to that.

"And what about crystals? No, there is no warmth there, and no life. But since the beginning of time every halite, or salt crystal has had four sides, and every quartz crystal has had six. Take snow crystals—like human beings and their fingerprints, no two have ever been found to be exactly alike. And yet, every snow crystal has six sides, and its planes are geometrically perfect, and always the same. Melt a snow crystal, and it is gone forever. Its unique pattern, as far as we know, will never appear again—just as a human being who dies will never appear again. You re-freeze the water of your melted crystal, just as human life may re-use elements that may once have been part of long dead ancestors—and what do you get? Another crystal, just as six-sided as the melted one—identical in its geometrical construction to the melted one. Yet, if only under the microscope, different in detail." The professor stopped a moment and looked at the two who were listening to him. When they remained silent, he continued.

"You can see the ancestry of my idea," he went on. "Perhaps not an accepted idea as yet, but a fundamentally practical one. I have been interested in what happens to the cells of the human body with the advent of cancer. We know that cancer is some kind of basic irritation of the body cells that starts them growing wildly in a way that may finally choke the normal functions of the organism, causing death.

"We also know that life itself may well be a kind of irritation—something that started with a special disturbance of certain organic molecules —something that touched them off on a chain reaction that wouldn't stop once it got started—made them follow their own sequence of chemical causes and effects that eventually resulted—well, in us."

"You think that crystals can be irritated then, like living cells?" David asked a little incredulously.

"I see you follow my line of reasoning," the professor said. "But, as a scientist, I don't think anything until I can prove it. I've worked with snow crystals, because I have found that I can manufacture them fairly easily in a little cold box I have devised here—introducing water vapor into a partially exhausted area at sub-zero temperature. And the snow crystal is subject to the same laws that govern any less easily manageable crystalline substance which couldn't be manufactured in perfect form in the laboratory. And I've had some interesting results.

"Certain impurities introduced into the crystal-making vapor," the professor went on, "caused reactions I didn't expect." He went over to one of the glassed-in cabinets and was about to open it, when he apparently thought better of it, and turned back to the other two.

"No matter. Whatever it was, the crystals I got from it seemed to be particularly hardy. Even when packed together, they failed to lose their individual identity under the microscope—even at a number of degrees above freezing. As a matter of fact, I noticed that if a large enough number of crystals were grouped together, those in the center of the group could apparently survive almost indefinitely temperatures up to fifty degrees.

"On a slide, individual crystals would melt as quickly as ordinary snow crystals. But put even a small group together on the slide, and they could maintain their shape up to forty degrees."

"And these are the crystals you used in your cloud-seeding experiment?" David asked.

"Well, I'm coming to that. As a matter of fact they were. But there was something else I noticed about the crystals resulting from this particular experiment. And this was the strangest thing of all. Once the crystals were formed, and kept in a cold place, they seemed to have a remarkable affinity for any water vapor present. I put some on a piece of wet blotting paper at about 35 degrees as a test. In ten minutes the blotting paper was completely dry within a radius of several centimeters. And something else rather remarkable. Under the microscope I noticed that the crystals on the blotting paper showed definite evidence of twinning."

"Twinning?" Karen asked.

"Mineralogical term which you've surely heard me use," the professor explained. "Twinning is what it's called when a mineral forms a double crystal with at least one—often more geometrical planes in common."

"Sort of like Siamese twins," Karen suggested.

"Same idea," the professor said. "As far as I know, and you can imagine I've looked into it rather intensively in the past couple of weeks, there has never been another example of snow crystals twinning."

"But you said there were impurities in these crystals of yours," David said. "What sort of impurities?"

The professor ignored the last half of his question. "Impurities, yes, but only in minute amounts—only enough to act as a catalytic agent. At least I must conclude the action was catalytic. There seemed to be no physical change in the crystals, that is, except . . ."

"Except what, Professor?"

"Except that under the microscope they seemed to have an unusual degree of almost diamond-like brilliance. But of course that may have just been the lighting in the microscope. That does happen sometimes.

"But, about the cloud-seeding. I couldn't resist trying them. I had no scientific reason to believe anything would happen actually. I was merely curious. So I injected a small test tube of them into the silver iodide spray I shot from the plane.

"It was only when I heard about the snow that I became frightened. I was afraid my crystals, with their affinity for moisture, might after all have started something in the upper air where it was cold enough for them to survive individually. I reasoned that if they had actually been able to start a storm—just a handful of crystals—the ultimate effect might turn out to be more than I bargained for. And I'm afraid I felt rather guilty and irresponsible for having tried them without further experimentation.

"You see," he took off his spectacles and wiped them with a pocket handkerchief, "I thought of my discovery only in terms of something that had happened in the laboratory—something that, since I wasn't working with dangerous materials, couldn't be dangerous."

"But it did turn out to be dangerous after all," David said.

The professor shrugged. "Well, I certainly was afraid it might until it stopped snowing. I really hadn't considered carefully enough what its effect might be in the proper atmospheric conditions. But I see now that I need not have worried. It's fairly obvious the snowstorm we are having at the moment is much too general and too well backed up by the weather reports to be traced to my crystals."

"Professor, aren't you forgetting the mouse on the table there?" Professor Cruickshank had seemed to regain his composure as he talked. Now, at David's question, his face grew tense again.

"No, I'm not forgetting the mouse, Mr. Storm. I confess I got rather a bad shock when you first showed me the mouse. You can understand why. You saw what my crystals had done to the piece of bacon in the dish. The coincidence struck me momentarily as one with very frightening implications."

"I should think it might, Professor—considering that a man was found dead this morning—killed apparently by the same thing that killed the mouse, not to mention a dog and a couple of dozen chickens."

Karen was looking at her father as though he had whipped her. "Oh, Dad, you don't think there could be . . ."

"That's the logical conclusion to draw, isn't it?" her father said bitterly. "My laboratory crystals draw the moisture out of a small fragment of bacon in a petri dish here. At the same time, not far from here, a man is found dead—along with some mice, chickens and a dog—all apparently withered by some strong dehydrating agent." He turned suddenly and faced his daughter and David, his lean jaw set defiantly. "As a scientist what can I think? How can I explain such a ghastly and fantastic coincidence unless I assume that my experiments here have in some way been responsible for the death of a human being?"

"I have examined the mouse you brought. And I have no choice but to admit the same thing that consumed the bacon here could have theoretically had the same effect on that mouse—on any living tissue—even the face of that man you say died so horribly. I can't offer you any alternative explanation. And yet . . ." He planted both hands on the table, fists clenched, and leaned heavily upon them, looking down at the partially dissected mouse. "And yet such a thing is absolutely and incontestably impossible!"

Karen went to him and put an arm around his shoulder. "Oh, Dad, of course it's impossible. Nobody's blaming you!"

"Of course nobody's blaming you, Professor Cruickshank," David said, a little less convincingly than Karen. "At worst it was a horrible accident."

"Accident!" The professor straightened up and glared at him. "Accident, you say. Let me show you something, young man." He pushed Karen almost roughly aside. Then he went over to the freezer and opened it. After a moment he came back with a small glass vial, coated with frost on the outside.

"There are the crystals that consumed the bacon," he said. "You can see how few of them there are. My cold box can hardly compete with nature as a maker of snowstorms. It takes a great deal of time and work to make even this many crystals. It wasn't a very much larger quantity that I used in the cloud-seeding experiment.

"Together as they are in this test tube, these crystals apparently have, for some reason, an affinity for moisture similar to a strong acid or alkali. I wouldn't suggest putting your finger into this test tube and leaving it there any length of time. But . . ." Over Karen's startled cry of protest, he shook a small clot of the crystals onto his palm and rubbed them onto the back of his other hand. "Scatter them," he said, "and they are quite harmless, except insofar as they apparently affect free-floating water vapor in the atmosphere." He held out his hand for their inspection. It was a little red from the cold. At first the individual flakes clung like tiny stars against the redness. Then one by one they blurred and became drops of water.

"The crystals I dropped from the plane," he went on as he rubbed the back of his hand dry and replaced the vial in the freezer, "were scattered through the blast of a sort of aerosol bomb, like the kind you use against moths. They must have been immediately so scattered they couldn't have damaged the wing of a mosquito. As to the possibility of their doing damage to living tissue on the ground several miles from here and three days later—it isn't even an astronomical possibility." He came back from the freezer, still rubbing his hand. "Can't you see what a ridiculous idea that is?"

"Yet these things actually did happen," David said. "You've convinced me your crystals couldn't have had anything to do with it. Yet something did kill Bailey and the chickens, and the mice—the same way your crystals would have if they could. They didn't just die—not that way."

"What did the police and medical referee say?" Cruickshank asked. "Did you get a chance to find out?"

"They didn't have much to say. They were pretty frightened themselves." David explained about the imposed secrecy and the fact Bailey's death was to be listed officially as a heart attack. "But it was pretty horrible, Professor. Both Karen and I saw it." David stood up and ground out his cigarette. "Eliminating your crystals, Professor, have you any suggestion at all as to what might have happened?"

"No suggestion at all, I'm afraid." The professor was standing by one of the smaller windows now, looking out at the snow.

"But surely, Professor, you must have some . . ." The professor turned around and spoke in tones of carefully controlled irritation.

"Mr. Storm, I said I don't know. There are many things that happen in this world which even a biochemist can't explain. If this were not true there would be no need for biochemists."

David shrugged. "Let me ask you one thing, Professor. Perhaps I'm speaking out of turn, but I've heard—from Dwight among others—that you've been a bit worried about these experiments of yours for some time. And, well, you seemed pretty upset just now when you first looked at the mouse. Is there any reason—other than what you've told us, that is—why you should be worried about your experiments?"

"If there had been, I should have told you." The professor's voice was cold. "It's scarcely unnatural to be worried about work one undertakes as seriously as what I am doing here. I expect what I am doing may have very significant results one day—results that have nothing to do with snowstorms in Cainfield, or dead mice found in a snowdrift!"

"What sort of results, Professor? You said something about cancer?"

"That, I'm afraid, will have to remain my business for the moment, Mr. Storm." Behind their thick lenses, the professor's eyes turned the color of grey steel. "And now perhaps you understand why I have a laboratory way up here in the woods where I don't have to be constantly bothered by people who want to ask me questions."

Karen gave David a warning glance and came forward. "Dad, David didn't mean . . ."

"I don't care what he meant. I've explained what I'm doing couldn't possibly have anything to do with what's happening down in the valley. I don't know what more there is to say, unless—unless you're accusing me of murdering that man they found in the snow."

Karen came up and put her hands on her father's shoulders. "Oh, Dad, for heaven's sake don't be a goop!" Cruickshank continued to glower at David. But his shoulders relaxed a little under his daughter's hands.

"I'm sorry, Karen," he said in a mollified voice, "but you know I don't like to be disturbed up here when I'm working. You two had better start on home before you get snowed in. I have a lot to do still."

"Dad, you're not going to stay up here all alone in weather like this." Karen looked at him sternly. Gently he lowered her hands from his shoulders.

"I'm sorry, my dear, but I'm afraid I must. You know I'm quite safe and comfortable here." He managed a smile. "And quite happy too." He turned to David. "Forgive me for being so rude just now, Mr. Storm. My daughter will undoubtedly explain to you as soon as my back is turned that I'm just a crotchety and harmless old man, and one shouldn't pay any attention to anything I say." He clapped a hand with unexpected vigor on David's shoulder. "Thanks for bringing your specimen. I'll want to study it further. Perhaps I can come up with something after all." He turned to Karen who was watching him anxiously. "Don't worry about me, my dear. I should be home tomorrow afternoon."

She looked at him doubtfully. "Dad, are you sure everything's all right?"

"Of course everything's all right."

Upstairs at the outside door the professor pulled Karen to him and kissed her gently on the forehead. "I may have the answer to a lot of things by tomorrow night," he said. She looked at him doubtfully a moment, then smiled and stepped out into the snow. As David moved to follow her, Cruickshank laid a hand on his arm. "I know what I'm doing," he said in a low voice.

David looked at him, momentarily surprised. Then he answered the professor's smile and they shook hands.

As he groped his way with Karen across the turnaround to the car, they both glanced back once or twice at the door where her father stood watching, framed in the light from the room behind. Then she took his hand as she heard the door behind them close at last.

David held her hand in silence till they reached the car. Cruickshank undoubtedly knew what he was doing, he thought. But what was he doing? It would be ridiculous, he thought, to look for any sinister intent in the professor's work at the old mill. Karen's father was perfectly sane, and he was neither irresponsible nor criminal. His explanation of why the laboratory crystals could not have caused the deaths of Bailey and the Gorts' chickens seemed logical and irrefutable—aside from the fact it was fantastic even to suspect such a thing.

And yet Bailey and the chickens—and to make it even more senseless, a handful of field mice—were dead. And Cruickshank had obviously been horrified to discover the similarity between the mysterious thing that killed them and what his laboratory crystals theoretically could do—provided it were possible to concentrate enough of them in the right place at the right time.

That would be like trying to find a way of causing a flood with a single tumbler of water, David thought, or—another thought came to him—like starting a fire with a match. He looked at Karen, sitting beside him, also lost in thought, and wished the idea of the match hadn't occurred to him. But he could not shut it from his mind, any more than he could forget what he had noticed when he shook hands with Karen's father in the doorway—that already there was an angry welt on the back of his hand where he had rubbed the snow crystals into it.

12 . . .

"PULL THE Goddam window down, Polly!" Duke LeBeau said thickly, "here it comes!" The girl beside him in the front seat of the car cranked down the window on her side, admitting a flurry of wind-driven snow. Duke, steering the car up the winding, snow-covered road with one hand, flipped a beer can past her face and out the window with the other. The can missed the yellow curve sign with its black bent arrow by inches.

"You stink," she said.

"Snowin' too hard." Without looking down, as he steered the car through the whirling opaque whiteness, he plunged his hand into the paper bag on the seat between them and brought out another can of beer. "Fix it for me, huh, honey?"

She groped for an opener in the glove compartment and did as he requested, a fine spray of beer showering them both as the opener point squeaked through the copper. "Where you get this stuff on Sunday?" she asked.

"Same place the old man does. He'll be down there gettin' himself p-a'ed right now."

"You sure it's OK. You sure he won't be home or anything?"

Duke held the beer can she had opened for him to his lips and tilted his head back as he drove. "Not so he can see anything if he is. He won't know what time it is till Monday morning. Same thing every Goddam weekend since Ma walked out on him two years ago—I tell you, honey, you can depend on the old man."

"How come you ain't brought me over before Sundays then?"

"Well, I tell you, honey, I been meanin' to ever since we both been workin' in the same shop. Kinda busy though. Guy has to kinda budget his time."

"Yeah, I bet. You ain't so busy though, I guess, big shot. Unless maybe you just talkin' big."

"Guess maybe I can do more than talk." He reached for her, taking his eyes off the road. But she slapped his hand down.

"You're driving a car, wise guy," she said. He spun the wheel just in time to make a right turn at the Westover corner. Angry at almost missing the turn, he thrust his foot down hard on the gas and the car slewed forward protestingly. They hadn't gone more than a few hundred yards when a spray of snow blinded the windshield. The car lurched sickeningly as its forward momentum met sudden soft resistance. As Duke jammed on the brake, it swung sidewise to the left, tilted up on two wheels for a moment, and came suddenly to rest. The jolt of stopping threw the girl against him. After the car had stopped, she remained where she was, and looked up at him expectantly. "Well, you ain't drivin' a car now," she said.

"We hit a snowdrift, baby," he announced, his voice thicker than it had been. He let her guide his arm around her. "This is a hell of a Goddam time of year to hit a snowdrift," he continued, not paying much attention to where his arm was. The meaning of his own words seemed to occur to him only after he had spoken them. He pushed her roughly back to her side of the car. "Gotta get out of the snowdrift," he said. "Can't do anything till we get out of the snowdrift, baby." He groped for the door handle, and stumbled out into the snow, slamming the door behind him.

She rubbed the inside of the steamed-up windshield, and could see him plainly as he went unsteadily around to the front of the car. Then, automatically, she reached for her purse, and began fixing her lips, using the rear-view mirror. Halfway through the ritual business, she stopped suddenly and listened. Then she edged over under the wheel and opened the window on his side. "You say somethin', honey?" she called. But she heard nothing except the soft sandy whisper of the snow on the windshield.

She could see him through the windshield though. He was leaning forward over the front of the hood, his hands spread out on it as if he were trying to embrace it. He seemed to be looking in her direction, and there was a silly expression on his face. She thought he was trying to say something, but she couldn't hear through the glass. She leaned forward and rubbed the glass again. He seemed to be singing now. His head was thrown back, and she could hear him faintly. Then suddenly he disappeared from sight down below the front of the hood.

She cursed him softly under her breath and opened the door. "Duke," she called. "Hey, Duke!" But there was no answer. "Hell of a Goddam time to pass out!" she said aloud and stepped out into the snow. It came above her knees and bit her legs sharply through the sheer stockings.

She pushed her way towards the front of the car where the snow had drifted even deeper. And then for a moment she forgot the burning cold of the snow on her legs. There was no sign of Duke. But the surface of the snow was shifting and jerking like a blanket covering a restless sleeper.

"Duke!" She sank to her knees in the soft drift and began digging like a rabbit with her bare hands . . .

Chief Carmichael leaned back in his swivel chair in the Cainfield police headquarters and tugged thoughtfully at his suspenders. "So the guy did die of heart failure after all," he said, looking at Dwight Heron and Sheriff McEwen who were sprawled in chairs across the small office, their legs stretched out in front of them.

"Most people do one way or another," Dwight Heron observed, his double chin settled comfortably on his chest. "That all Doc Markel had to say when he called?"

"Just about." Carmichael rocked his chair thoughtfully a moment. "Said Bailey had come in for a routine check once couple of months back, and he hadn't found any reason to suspect heart trouble. 'Course you can't ever tell with a man that age."

"What about the dehydration?" McEwen asked. "What made his face look like that?"

"Says he don't know. No way to tell. All he knows is most of it happened after the guy was dead."

McEwen shook his head slowly. "That don't shed any great light on the situation from where I sit. What do you make of it, Dwight?"

Heron sighed. "From what you guys have told me, I don't even know where to begin. Got any ideas what you're going to do about it?"

McEwen shrugged. "Put the guy in a box quick as we can get him there, I guess, and file a report in Concord."

"Lucky he doesn't have any relatives around who'll want to take a last look," Carmichael put in.

"Matter of fact," McEwen said, "we're going to have more trouble about those chickens than we did with Bailey. Going to be mighty tough explaining to anyone around this town those eighteen chickens died of heart failure."

Carmichael's chair groaned as he sat up. "Well," he said, "Callan sure as hell can't find anything else they died of, except something drained all the juice out of 'em. No disease."

"And this started out to be such a nice quiet Sunday," McEwen sighed.

Stomping the snow from their boots as they came in the door, David and Karen found the three sitting in morose silence.

"Just beginning to wonder where you chillun had taken yourselves off to," Dwight said, hauling himself to his feet as they came in. "Come in and join the wake. Or have you solved the case so we can all go home?"

"We thought probably you people had. That's why we dropped in," David said. "Any word on Bailey yet?" Carmichael told him what Markel had said on the phone. "So what now?" he asked.

McEwen gave him a baleful look. "You got any ideas, Mr. Storm?"

"No, but I've got something to add to the confusion." He told about the field mice the biologist from Concord had discovered.

"Oh, Jesus Christ," McEwen groaned. "You sure it's the same thing?"

"Looks like it." McEwen looked at Carmichael.

"Well, that's something to work on at least," he said.

"What's the guy's name?" Carmichael asked.

"Manning, I think. He's at the Waverton." Carmichael reached for the phone on his desk. It rang before he could pick it up.

"Police Department, Carmichael," he said automatically. He grew suddenly tense as he listened. "Take it easy, mister," he said into the phone after a moment. "Just try to tell me what happened." Then he listened again, his eyes widening. His face, as it had been when Bailey was discovered, turned from red to mottled purple. "OK," he said finally. "Stay right where you are till we get there." He put the phone back in its cradle, almost as if he were afraid of it, and sat for a moment staring straight ahead of him.

"Guy and a girl dead alongside their car on Barker Mountain road up near Westover corner," he said finally with an effort. "Guy who called was pretty hysterical. Hard to tell from what he said . . ." He looked at the others, fear showing frankly in his eyes.

"We'd better call the state police. It looks like the same thing that happened to Bailey."

13 . . .

DAVID AND KAREN followed Carmichael's cruiser to the scene in Heron's car which was better equipped to keep up the pace than the ancient Chevrolet. Dwight drove in tight-lipped silence. David sat with his arm around Karen, staring straight ahead at the snowflakes that seemed to be flying upwards into the windshield. He could feel her trembling.

Two state police cars had already arrived when they pulled up finally behind Carmichael's cruiser, and a green-uniformed state trooper came up and peered in the window.

"Press," Dwight said.

"Oh, it's you, Heron. Didn't recognize you," the trooper said. "Better not let the lady go up there."

"That's right, darling," David said. "You'd better stay here."

She looked at him pleadingly. "David, don't leave me alone."

"You'll be all right." He laid his hand gently against her cheek.

"Don't be gone long, David. I'm scared." He kissed her, and she managed a faint smile as he backed out the door. Then he followed Dwight, Carmichael, McEwen and the trooper up the road.

Two other troopers were talking to a thin, small man in a trenchcoat whose face was grey-green with fright. Beyond the group a small two-door sedan stood at an angle to the road, its back end swung out to the left so that the road was almost blocked. Near the front end two tarpaulins were spread over the trampled snow, and there was something under each of them.

One of the troopers who had been talking with the man in a trench-coat came over and nodded to Carmichael and McEwen. McEwen introduced him to Dwight and David as Lt. Haugsrud of the state police.

"Suppose you'll want to take a look," Haugsrud said to McEwen. "I warn you, it's pretty rough." McEwen nodded. As the four of them gathered closer, Haugsrud pulled back a corner of first one tarpaulin, then the other.

Mercifully, the girl was lying face down, and her features were hidden under her disarranged hair. But one arm was flung out as if reaching towards the other tarpaulin. David saw the clenched fist. And he saw the face of the man, staring sightlessly skyward just like Bailey. Both figures were covered with a light powdering of snow. No second glance was necessary to see that both had suffered the same fate as Bailey. Only this time it looked even worse. From what David could see, there wasn't as much left this time. He turned away, feeling sick till Haugsrud dropped the tarpaulins back in place.

"We've identified them both," Haugsrud said in a subdued voice. "According to his driver's license, the man is Geoffrion LeBeau of Cainfield. Know him, Os?" He turned to Carmichael.

"Duke LeBeau? Sure. Lives just down the road here. Works over in White River Junction."

"That him?" Haugsrud nodded towards the nearest of the tarpaulins.

Carmichael shifted uncomfortably. "Hard to tell now. Couldn't say it wasn't."

"Well, no reason to think it's anybody else. Found letters in the girl's purse addressed to Polly Carpenter in White River Junction, so that figures. Doc Markel coming?"

Carmichael nodded. "Any minute. He's been tied up. We had another like this just this morning, less than half a mile from here."

"You *what?*" Haugsrud turned to McEwen. Briefly McEwen explained about Bailey and the chickens. Haugsrud listened, his lips pursed in a silent whistle.

"Heart failure or no heart failure, looks like you should have called us sooner, McEwen."

"Looks that way. Don't know what more you could have done than we did, though," McEwen said grimly. "What happened this time?"

"Let you talk to this guy over here." He nodded towards the man in the trenchcoat who was still talking with the other trooper, and the group moved over.

The man in the trenchcoat looked at them with haunted eyes. "Honestly," he said, "I don't know anything about it, I . . ."

"We're not accusing you of anything," Haugsrud said almost gently. "Just take it easy and tell the sheriff and the Chief here how you found them."

In an unsteady voice the man explained that he lived in Framingham, Massachusetts, and had been visiting relatives in Warren. On the way back he had got lost in the storm and had taken the wrong turn at the crossroads. "Then I saw this car just the way it is now, halfway across the road. I thought maybe there'd been an accident. So I pulled up behind it and got out. It was snowing pretty hard. I didn't see them until I almost stumbled over—over the woman. She was half covered with snow. And the wind seemed to be blowing the snow away in a sort of cloud.

"I must have stood there a minute just staring at her. And while I stood there the wind blew more snow off her, and I could see . . ." He broke off, looking from one to the other of the still faces in the group around him. "I saw the other one then—just his face through the snow. I guess I don't remember much after that except I got in my car and headed for the nearest farm to call up. Please, can I go now? I'm late, I . . ."

"We'll all be going down town in a few minutes," Haugsrud said. "You can get some coffee then, and we may need to ask you a few more questions. Then you can go. Know how you feel," he said as an afterthought.

David had watched the proceedings so far in a growing torment of indecision. He realized that he knew more than any of the others standing around him about what was happening—more than the others would ever learn unless they talked to Professor Cruickshank, or Cruickshank came to them. And yet what did he know? There was nothing that could be proved and demonstrated. All he knew was that there was a dreadful fear in the back of his mind that could not be put in any kind of words that wouldn't sound like sheerest hysteria.

Already McEwen and Carmichael had rejected his theory of something in the snow—even the theory of something remotely possible, like pollution from the air. But perhaps they would think differently now that two more people were dead.

"Have you looked at your shoes since you were standing in the snow?" David asked the man who had found the bodies.

"Shoes?" The man looked at him uncomprehendingly. David felt the faces of the others turned towards him.

"What's on your mind, son?" Haugsrud looked at David narrowly. "You know something about this?"

"Mr. Storm was there when we found Bailey this morning," McEwen put in. "Maybe we'd better ask the gentleman to show us his shoes."

Haugsrud looked puzzled for a moment, then shrugged. "You better stick around," he told David. Then he turned to the man in the trench-coat. "Would you mind?" he asked.

"I don't get it," the man said tremulously. But he leaned a hand against the police cruiser behind him and raised one leg. He was wearing low oxfords with rubbers. David saw that the rubber all along the sides had worn or been peeled off, exposing the canvas underneath. He turned quickly to Dwight, who was standing beside him.

"Dwight," he said quickly, "do me a favor and take Karen home in your car. Tell her everything's all right and I'll explain later."

"Dave-boy," Dwight said, "you holding out on us? What is this?"

"Look, Dwight, I'll explain everything later. Just a theory of mine— might be something."

"Won't get yourself in trouble?"

"Hope not."

Dwight looked at him queerly for a moment, then clapped him on the shoulder. "Call me when you get back, Dave." He turned and lumbered off towards the car where Karen was.

The man in the trenchcoat was still looking at the mutilated rubber. "I tell you," he said, "they were brand new last week. They weren't like that when I put them on this morning." Instinctively each of the others in the group looked at his own shoes and found no damage.

McEwen's eyes went from the damaged rubber to David and back again. "By God, maybe you had something this morning after all, Storm," he said.

"That what you were expecting, Storm?" Haugsrud asked.

"Something like that," David said.

"Maybe you'd better tell us about it."

"I'd better let the sheriff and Chief Carmichael do that," David said. "I just happened to be along." As McEwen outlined the story of what had happened that morning, David heard the sound of Heron's car start-ing up and turning. He looked up in time to see it disappearing down the road. He began to wish he hadn't mentioned the shoes, and had gone home with Karen. But he knew he would not have felt comfortable if he had. He would not have been able to get Bailey, or what he had seen under the tarpaulins out of his mind. She'd be all right with Dwight, and God knows, she'd had enough for one day.

"Storm's idea was that there was something in the snow that did this," McEwen was saying. "Some chemical, or . . ."

Haugsrud snorted. "Well, God damn it there's nothing in this snow here now. That's plain enough."

"No but apparently there was when this gentlman got here." David indicated the man in the trenchcoat, who was still studying his damaged footwear.

"Can't prove that, any more than we can prove that's what happened to them." He nodded towards the tarpaulins. "Besides, you got any idea what kind of a chemical might do that, and how it might get here—not only get here, but disappear after it had done its job?"

David admitted he hadn't. "But there's something else the sheriff didn't mention," he added. Then he told about the encounter with Manning, the microtus man from Concord, and about the mice Manning had showed him.

"You say it was near here where you pushed him out of the ditch?"

"Not more than a few hundred yards, I think." David peered down the road through the falling snow, trying to recollect landmarks.

"And you saw the mice?"

David nodded. "Same as this."

Haugsrud frowned thoughtfully. "Chemical or no chemical, we've damned sure got something on our hands around here. Where'd he find the mice, d'you know?"

"He said they'd been nibbling at the bark of some bushes along the road—like those over there." David nodded towards a clump of wild cherry bushes that grew about ten feet high just the other side of the ditch.

Haugsrud strolled over towards the bushes, then stopped suddenly and beckoned the others. "For mice," he said, "that's a mighty Goddam good job of nibbling."

David and the others came over. There was scarcely an inch of snow on the bank where the wild cherries grew. But as far as David could see on either side, every tree and bush on the bank had been stripped clean of bark for more than a foot above the snowline.

For a moment nobody moved or spoke. Then, through the falling snow, came the muffled wail of the police ambulance siren.

14 . . .

"LET ME GET this straight," Lt. Haugsrud said later after they had all gathered in the Cainfield police station. "After you had seen Bailey and the chickens, you remembered the pair of boots that had got chewed up on the Edgertons' side porch. And that's what made you think we ought to take a look at Mr. Hewitt's shoes. That right, Mr. Storm?" Haugsrud sat on a corner of Carmichael's desk looking at David with a quizzical frown.

David looked at the man in the trenchcoat, who was sitting in a chair against the wall, drinking coffee from a cardboard carton. "That's right," he said.

"That was a mighty sharp piece of deduction—either that or a hell of a long coincidence as it turned out. How'd you happen to think of that?"

David pulled up a chair next to McEwen, facing Carmichael's desk. "Well," he said, "I remember something Dr. Callan said this morning about the chickens—how their legs looked as if mice had been at them. When I saw the shoes, that's the way the shoes looked too. The shoes had been out in the snow—so had Bailey; so had the chickens . . ."

"The chickens were in the henhouse, weren't they?"

Carmichael, who had looked as though he were asleep in his swivel chair, looked up. "Yeah, but there was powder snow all over the floor of the henhouse—on the feathers, too."

"And then this afternoon," David went on, "I saw the two up there looking just like Bailey, and with the same powdery snow all over them

. . . and Mr. Hewitt here said he nearly stumbled over the girl. So I thought he must have got into whatever was in the snow at the time."

"Well, it looks as though you may have thought right," Haugsrud said. "But I'll be Goddamned if any of it makes sense!" He pulled off his visored cap and slammed it on the desk, running his other hand through his thinning blond hair. He glanced about the group as if expecting some sort of clarification. But none was forthcoming. Finally McEwen leaned forward in his chair, looking thoughtfully at the floor between his knees.

"Mr. Hewitt," he said, "do I understand you to say that the bodies were partially covered with snow when you found them?"

Hewitt glanced up nervously from his coffee. "That's right. Seemed to be sort of drifted around them."

"Drifted, Mr. Hewitt?" McEwen looked up at him. "Little early in the fall for snowdrifts, isn't it?"

"I know, but I tell you, I saw . . ."

"Mr. Hewitt, you were on your way down from Warren, you say. You must have had plenty of opportunity to notice how much snow there was on the roads. How much snow would you say had fallen by the time you found the bodies?"

"Why, I wouldn't say it looked like more than an inch or two . . ."

"And yet you say that the snow had drifted over the bodies. Not only that, you saw the wind was blowing the snow away from around the bodies when you got there?"

"That's right."

"Mr. Hewitt, did you notice the wind blowing up any snow clouds anywhere else?"

"No, I didn't notice it anywhere else."

"Of course you didn't notice it anywhere else! There hasn't been enough wind or enough snow all day to make the kind of drift that could cover a body—let alone blow it away afterwards! Yet you say the bodies were covered. And when we got there there was almost no snow around them—except for a little powder snow on their clothes!"

"Take it easy, Ed," Carmichael put in. "Don't forget it was the same thing with Bailey—hardly any snow around him. Even the footprints wiped out, as if maybe the wind had blown them away. Remember?"

McEwen sighed and looked at Carmichael, a look of desperation on his face. "And where do these Goddamned trees with no bark on 'em fit in?" he demanded. "You know, the deeper we get into this thing, the crazier it looks. And it doesn't look as though we'd get much more out of Doc Markel about this than we did with Bailey. Don't have to be a doctor to see *what* they died of! All we got to know is who or what did it, and how!" He got up nervously.

"That's all we got to know—how it happened. Simple enough, Mr. Storm tells us—something in the snow. I'll go along with that. What the hell else could it be? Something in the snow. *But, God damn it, what?*" His voice rose almost to a shout. For a moment his normally placid features were distorted with the same unreasoning fear of the unknown that had been a cold emptiness in the pit of David's stomach since he had first laid eyes on the still, horrible remnant of Bailey in the snow that morning.

A silent wave of McEwen's fear spread to the others, and they remained silent. Only Hewitt moved, slowly setting down his coffee container and raising his white face to stare at the sheriff, the horror of what he had seen that afternoon coming back into his eyes.

David looked at Haugsrud. "Need me any more right now?" he asked in a low voice.

Haugsrud shook his head. "Stay in touch," he said.

David slipped gratefully out of the room into the damp twilight. It had stopped snowing, and grey clouds scudded overhead, borne on a damp, chilling wind that stirred in the yellow leaves of the elms along the street. The street was almost deserted. But on the walks the snow had already been trodden to brown slush.

David climbed into his car, shivering under his field jacket in the unseasonable cold, and started the motor. Sunday with Karen, he thought ironically. How long ago the morning seemed when they had started out from Kelsey's and the sun was shining. He knew now he wanted to see Karen very badly.

"She's home," Dwight said. David had called from a drugstore the moment he got to Westover. "Asked her to come over and stay with us tonight, since she was going to be alone in the house. But she wanted to go home, so I sent Gloria over to spend the night with her. She's nervous and upset after today. Can't blame her. Good thing you asked me to take her home, I guess. You coming over to see me afterwards? Imagine you have lots to tell me."

David promised he would, and a few moments later he had pulled his car up in front of the house with the green shutters.

Gloria Heron, plump and benevolent-looking, almost a female counterpart of Dwight, met him at the door, wrapped in a voluminous housecoat. Her reading glasses were balanced on the end of her nose and she held an open book in her hand. "Well, David," she said, "I guess you've had a day of it. Come in."

"Hello, Gloria," he said. "How's Karen? Is she all right?"

"Of course she's all right. Why shouldn't she be? When last heard from she was upstairs taking a shower. You look all-in, Dave-boy. Plunk yourself down and take your shoes off or something." She went to the stairs. "Karen! Friend of yours down here panting for a drink, and I don't know where the hell you keep it—yes, it's David."

She turned back to David. "She'll be right along," she said. "In the meantime how about making with the gory details of what happened this afternoon." She led him towards the living-room and watched him sink down onto the sofa with a heavy sigh. "On second thought," she said, "I can see you'd rather not. Pretty bad, was it?" David nodded.

A moment later Karen burst into the room, clad in a terry-cloth bathrobe, her hair done up in a turban of towel. "Hi," she said breathlessly, "I wasn't expecting you for hours yet." She came up and kissed him lightly as he rose and took her extended hands. Then she looked at him in mock seriousness. "You stood me up this afternoon, so I was hoping they'd arrest you or something. Would have served you right, I . . ."

"Karen, I'm awfully sorry."

"Don't be a goop! Good thing you did send me home. I was beginning to get a bad case of the willies anyhow."

"Well, if you kids will excuse me," Gloria said, "I've got a date with Winston Churchill's war memoirs—volume three."

"Shall I wake you at suppertime?" Karen asked.

"No hurry. I'll raid the icebox later. Be seeing you." Gloria went upstairs.

"Oh, Dave," Karen said, "it's good to see you." She ran a hand into his hair. "But you look beat. Come on in the kitchen and I'll show you where the fixings are." She took his hand and pulled him towards the kitchen. "You can whip up martinis while I change. You could light the fire in the living-room too if you like . . ." She scurried about in the kitchen, rattling drawers and cupboards to get the necessary glasses and equipment. He caught her and pulled her to him.

"Hey," he said, "you're all wound up, darling."

She shook her head. "Just glad to see you." Then she broke away from him and ran upstairs to change.

A few minutes later they were seated on the couch in the living-room in front of the fire, Karen in a blue housecoat minus turban. She seemed calmer since she had come back downstairs. "To our Sundays," she said. "And let's hope they aren't all like this one." They clinked glasses. She sipped hers and put it down, suddenly serious. "Really awful, Dave?"

He nodded. "Not so much what happened. I've seen worse than that. It was the way the sheriff and the police and all of them bustled around making official noises and everything and going through all the proper procedures and questions. And all the time they were scared to death and knew they were up against something completely beyond them."

"Why did you stay, Dave, if it was so awful?"

"I guess I had to. I knew a few things they didn't."

"You didn't bring Dad into it?"

"No."

"I'm glad you didn't." She laid her hand on his.

"It was more than what I had to tell them—why I stayed. I guess I was afraid too. I had to see it for myself, so I could try to explain it to myself."

"And could you?" He shook his head. "David, what is it they're up against? Do you know? Do you have any ideas?"

He got up and walked to the fireplace. "I wish I did. I wish I didn't have the feeling it was something that was only just beginning. Something that . . ." He stopped, seeing the look in her eyes. "Now I've frightened you." He came back to the sofa and took her hands. "Oh, darling, let's not talk about it, for tonight at least. It's something that doesn't even belong in the same world you live in. When I look at you, I know such things are impossible and can't be."

"Why when you look at me?"

"Because when I look at you I know it's outrageous for snow to be anything but nice clean white stuff kids make snowballs out of—ordinary snowballs that don't get bigger all by themselves, and don't hurt their hands."

She reached out and touched his hair with the tips of her fingers. "You're tired, darling," she said.

"I'm also in love with you."

"Oh, Dave!" She was suddenly in his arms, her face against his chest, clinging to him hard. "Hold me close, I'm frightened."

[84]

"Why should you be frightened?"

"Because . . . because you are."

"Not any more. That the only reason?"

She clung to him still. "No," she said.

"What is it, then?"

"Oh, Dave, take me away from here!"

He raised her gently and looked at her. "What is it you want me to take you away from, Karen?"

She lowered her head to avoid his eyes. "I don't know."

"Anything to do with your father?"

She looked at him, her eyes wide and grey. She looked as if she wanted to say something. Finally she lowered her eyes again. "I'm sorry," she said. "I think I love you too, Dave." She straightened up suddenly and picked up her martini. "But I've just got the creeps after today. Don't ask me to talk about anything tonight."

He picked up his own glass and held it, studying the floating twist of lemon peel. "OK, but sometimes it's better to talk."

"I can't, Dave. Not even to you."

"You've always been pretty close to your father, haven't you?"

"Sometimes," she said. "I'd like to be, yes. But Dad's never let anyone get close to him since Mother died. He needs me to cook his meals and pick up after him. He'd fall apart if I weren't around. But he lives in his own little world, and I don't belong there most of the time. Sometimes I think he even hates me when I intrude on him. And then, sometimes, I suppose because I remind him of Mother, he has to talk to me about things. And afterwards he always wishes he hadn't."

"Maybe you shouldn't stay here then, Karen."

"What else can I do?"

"He could hire someone to keep house for him."

"He wouldn't, Dave."

"What is this little world of his, Karen? His research up at the lab?"

"His research and whatever it is he thinks about up there."

"Is he really working on something to do with cancer?"

"He says so. And then, when he feels like talking, he tells me a lot of strange things that don't make sense."

"Such as . . ."

She looked at him pleadingly. "Oh, Dave, what does it matter! I wish we could get him interested in helping the police with what's happened. He could help them, I'm sure, if anybody could. And it might bring him out of himself. But I'm afraid, Dave . . . I'm afraid of what he might tell them."

"Is there something he shouldn't tell them?"

"Of course not. But you know how he was about the snow. How he thought it would go on and on snowing because of his rain-making experiments. And that it would be all his fault if it did? I'm afraid he might take it into his head to blame himself for what's happened in Cainfield. After all, it is a coincidence that he's working with snow crystals."

David set down his glass and stared into the fire. "Karen, do you think there's any chance he might be to blame—unintentionally, I mean?"

"Darling, Dad is one of the best biochemists in the country. But he isn't a magician. And he wouldn't dream of hurting anybody, or even taking a chance of hurting anybody."

"Then why would he want to blame himself for the things that have been happening there? He certainly denied responsibility for it today up at the lab."

"Yes, I know. But you should hear some of the things he's told me and then tried to pretend afterwards he hadn't told me. He'd like to blame himself for something like that as a sort of punishment."

"I don't understand."

"Mother died of cancer—quite painfully. Dad loved her very much. The ordeal of watching her suffer without being able to do anything to help her was almost too much for him. He'd been working on his cancer experiments. And, I suppose because he hadn't found a cure for cancer in time to save her, he blamed himself for her death."

David reached over and took her hand. "And that's why he wants to punish himself?"

"I think so." David put his arm around her and pulled her close to him. For a while they were both silent, watching the fire. "You know," she said finally, "I told you I thought his fear that it would go on snowing indefinitely in Cainfield was just something he invented. David, I don't believe he has any snow crystals either—not that can do the things he says. I think he just got the idea from what happened in Cainfield."

David, his arm still around her, turned to look at her. She was staring straight ahead of her into the fire.

"What makes you think that, Karen?" he asked. He was thinking of the welt on the back of her father's hand.

"I . . . I just know, David."

"He shouldn't be up there alone if that's the way it is," David said.

"I know. But it would be worse to try and stop him from going there."
She turned to him. "What can I do?"

He looked at her searchingly a moment, then he kissed her lightly
on the lips. "I'll tell you what you can do," he said, "you can fix us some
supper."

A little later he stood watching her as she broke spaghetti into a pot of
boiling water. "Darling, one thing," he said. "What sort of things did
your father tell you?"

"Oh . . . he told me once he thought he had discovered the secret of
life." She dropped the rest of the spaghetti into the water and reached
for the salt.

15 . . .

KAREN WAS TIRED and made no objection when David said he had to leave early. But she clung to him a moment at the door. "I hope you meant it when you said you loved me," she said. "That's awfully important. I need you, Dave."

He kissed her. "It's important you get some sleep, too."

"Dave . . . You do believe me about my father?" She looked at him earnestly.

"Karen . . . of course I do. Try not to worry too much. I'll see you tomorrow." He kissed her again and went to his car. As he drove off he looked back once and saw her still standing in the doorway, looking after him.

It was only a little after nine when he reached Dwight's. The Herons lived in a remodelled colonial vintage farmhouse on the edge of town that had a wide, neatly kept lawn and a barn that had long since ceased to be functional, except as a garage and workshop. Some snow had fallen in Westover too, and the thinly covered lawn gleamed under the porch light as David drove up.

Dwight met him at the door in shirtsleeves, a bottle of beer in one hand. "Beginning to think you weren't coming. Karen and Gloria behaving themselves all right?"

"I guess so."

"Grab yourself a beer in the icebox, Dave-boy, and start talking. I want to know what you had up your sleeve this afternoon. You really rushed us off in a hurry."

"Oh, I guess I didn't have anything much as it turns out," David said when he had settled himself in an armchair facing Dwight, a perspiring bottle balanced on his knee. "Guess I was mostly worried about Karen. Didn't want her waiting around in case I got involved."

"How involved did you get?" David told him all that had happened. "Well, maybe my theory isn't much," he concluded. "But at least it's as good as anything the sheriff and the police have. They're scared to death and don't even know where to start."

Dwight settled down deeper in his chair, hooking a leg over one of its upholstered arms. "Just exactly what is your theory, Dave? Maybe we'd get somewhere if you tried to tell me in so many words—and where you don't *know* what happened, fill in with what you *think* happened."

"Good idea. Got a map of Cainfield?"

With a groan, Dwight hoisted his bulk out of the chair and went to a glassed-in bookcase. In a moment he came back with a rolled-up geological survey map. "You want to grab the card-table over there behind the door?" They pulled up their chairs and weighted the unrolled map on the table with ash trays. David took out a pencil.

"Well, first of all," he said, "we have a freak snowstorm in Cainfield covering about this much area." He drew a wide circle around Cainfield on the map. "Now, assuming the snow had something to do with what's to come, what's the first thing that happened? A pair of shoes left out on a snow-covered porch start to disintegrate. That would be here." He located the crossroads north of the town and put an "x" on the tiny black square indicating the Edgertons' house. "Next, Robin Gort hurts his hands playing in the snow just across the road—here." He made another "x." "For all we know," he added, "Robin may just have been suffering from poison ivy. But let's assume for the moment that the snow—or something in it—is responsible for everything that happened, crazy as that sounds.

"So, Robin makes a snowball. Just to include everything, he tells us it got bigger all by itself. No way of proving that's anything but childish imagination of course. But while the Gorts are away that night, the snowball apparently rolls down the hill and hits the henhouse—here." He made another "x" right next to the other. "In the morning all the chickens are found mysteriously dead, and it's obvious there's been snow in the henhouse. But there's nothing left of it except a little bit of powder.

"Later that morning, we find Bailey mysteriously dead about here." He added still another "x." "Same thing. All shrivelled up, just like the chickens—covered with powder snow, but not much snow around him. Same with Bailey's dog.

"Next we come to where I gave the biologist from Concord a push. Presumably he found his dead mice—withered in the same way—in this same area." He made another "x" on the road to the Westover corner. "Not more than a hundred yards or so from this point we come to the place where the bodies were found this afternoon. Same thing all over again—this time with a witness to testify he saw snow which had been covering the bodies, being blown away—and by a wind that wasn't strong enough apparently to drift the snow anywhere else. The car and the bodies were about here." He made a final "x." "And the bark was eaten off the trees on both sides of the road in an area about this wide." He made two parallel lines across the road, one on each side of the final "x."

"Now, a couple of things that seem to be common to each incident: whatever is dangerous in the snow doesn't seem to stay where it is. Once the snow which apparently covers the victim to start with is blown away, what's left isn't dangerous. The witness this afternoon, who was the only person yet to come across any of the victims *before* the snow had blown away, was the only one who suffered any damage to his footwear.

"Another thing: whatever this is we're after, it seems to be very particular about what it consumes and what it doesn't. It seems to absorb the moisture from living tissue, and eats the bark off trees. It also seems to damage both rubber and leather. But it doesn't harm cloth, hair or feathers.

"Now we come to the strangest damn thing of all," David said. Dwight looked up from the map, an expression of awe already on his face. "Connect up the crosses we have on the map. We have a line, maybe two miles long, curving from west to northwest. Now, how often does the wind blow from the east around here?"

"Not very often, except when we have a northeaster."

"Exactly. Now, best I can remember—we can easily check it with weather reports—the wind yesterday and today was coming generally from the northwest. Dwight . . ." David looked squarely into the other's eyes, "whatever this Goddam thing is, it was drifting west—*directly against the wind!*"

Dwight stared at him a moment and then whistled softly. "Hell of a nice job of summing up, Dave. Too damned good. You scare the hell out of me!" David was silent while he finished his beer.

"You tell the police all this?" Dwight asked.

David shook his head. "Not just like that. They've got all the same information. They'll figure it out the same way, I guess, once they get over their jitters and stop worrying about what the newspapers are going to do to them."

"Hell of a lot of good it will do them if they do! What do we know, even with your outline? Nothing, except that such a thing just plain isn't possible. And yet, it's happening."

"One thing we can wonder about," David said, "is where it's going from here."

Dwight looked at the map. "Looks like Barker Mountain if it stays on course."

"But if it can sail against the wind, we haven't any guarantee that it will stay on course. Dwight, I have a feeling we haven't seen anything yet."

"On that cheerful note," Dwight said, "I need another beer." He rose and David followed him as he lumbered into the kitchen. Taking the fresh bottle Dwight handed him, he leaned against the refrigerator, while Dwight stoked more bottles from a cardboard case on the floor into the ice compartment.

"Dwight," he asked, "do you think Professor Cruickshank could help us with this?" Dwight stopped what he was doing and looked up at him. "I mean, he's working with snow crystals. I should think he might have some theories."

"I imagine he's got some theories, all right." Dwight stood up laboriously. "Don't think you'd get him to help, though."

"You know Karen and I saw him up in the lab this noon."

Dwight looked genuinely surprised. "No kidding! Karen didn't tell me anything about that. You must rate. I've never been up there myself. How'd you happen to do that?"

"Took him one of the mice that guy Manning from Concord found. Thought he might be able to tell us something about what killed it."

"Did he?"

"That's the funny thing, Dwight," David said as they walked back to the living-room. "He didn't seem to know any more than Dr. Markel did. But he seemed very upset about it at first."

"How so?"

"Well, you remember the snow crystals he was talking about the other night. Seems they do some very peculiar things. He showed me a piece of bacon rind. There wasn't much left of it. Crystals ate it, he said."

"Oh, Jesus Christ, no . . . !" Dwight looked at him in momentary horror. "Dave, you aren't trying to suggest . . ."

"I confess I thought of it. Cruickshank himself says it couldn't possibly have caused anything that happened outside. And, somehow, I believe him."

"I should hope. Never occurred to me to make the connection after what he told us about his 'snowstorm' at dinner the other night. Frankly, it still doesn't occur to me. Nathan's an old friend, Dave."

David sat down in his chair again, feeling uncomfortable about what he knew he had to say next.

"Dwight," he began, "just between us, is there any chance Karen's father is for some reason just inventing all this about the crystals? That he really hasn't discovered anything of the sort?" Dwight looked at him sharply.

"Why in the name of hell and thunderation would he bother to do a thing like that? Where'd you get that idea?"

"From Karen."

"From Karen!" Dwight stared at him.

"She told me just this evening." David realized suddenly he didn't quite know how to explain to Dwight what Karen had told him. "She said he might have reasons to . . . to . . ."

Dwight shrugged. "Nathan does like to dramatize himself a bit. But it seems hard to imagine he would go that far."

"That's what I thought," David said. "But why would Karen say a thing like that if it wasn't—if it wasn't true."

"Karen ought to know," Dwight said, frowning at his bottle of beer. "Karen ought to know better than we do."

"But, Dwight, I know he's got the crystals." David explained about the welt that had appeared on Cruickshank's hand after rubbing it with the snow from the test tube.

Dwight listened to this in silence, working on his bottle of beer. "You know something," he said. "I have an idea we ought to get Nathan's opinion on all this after all. Maybe there are a few things I'd like to ask him myself."

"He said he'd be back tomorrow afternoon."

"Hell, why wait till tomorrow afternoon? What's the matter with right now? Nathan never goes to bed. If I know him he'll be up puttering around that lab of his."

"You serious?"

"As I've told you before, Dave-boy, I'm always serious. I don't give a damn if you believe what I tell you about Nathan. But if you got any doubts about what Karen told you, it's time we got them straightened out. She's a swell girl, Dave, and she's fallen for you pretty hard.

"Besides," he said, chuckling a little, "I'd kind of like to catch that old bastard by surprise for once and see just exactly what he does in that lab of his."

"We'll take my car. Guess we got time for another beer first."

16...

HALFWAY BETWEEN the Westover corner and the crossroads where the Gorts lived, a narrow dirt road ran northward a quarter of a mile across open field and pastureland to the farm of Willis Foss. The fields and pasture belonged to Foss all the way to the main road. But the farm itself was set right up against the slope of Barker Mountain. And the hard-wood forest that covered the mountain slope began the other side of a stone wall only a hundred feet behind the barn.

Willis Foss was a leather-faced giant of a man, well past his sixtieth birthday, but lean and muscular still as a man of forty. He belonged to the rapidly dwindling New England puritan stock that still has a twang of Elizabethan England in its speech. He liked living so far off the main road where he didn't have to see or talk to anyone but his family if he didn't want to. And he was an orderly man, who loved to have everything in its fitting and proper place—even the seasons.

As he carried his lantern to the barn at eight o'clock before going to bed, the damp cold pierced his thick wool shirt uncomfortably. The wet snow in the barnyard splatted under his feet. It wasn't the right weather for the time of the year. He could hear the leaves rustling in the maples behind the barn—not a dry rustle, like oak leaves in winter—but soft, like summer leaves. And the pasture would be green enough for the stock for some weeks yet—if it didn't snow any more. The cold, and the wet snow, made him feel uneasy. Maybe he was just getting old, he thought. He didn't like to think of that.

[94]

The warm, acrid-sweet air of the barn struck him as he rolled the sliding door back, and he heard the shifting and heavy breathing of the cattle in their stanchions. Now and then a stanchion rattled and creaked as the occupant made a sudden movement, or bent down to feed. They're restless too, he thought. Guess they're feeling the weather like me.

The chickens clucked sleepily as he opened the door. Nothing likely to get in here, he thought. Built solid as the main house. Too bad about the Gorts' chickens. Nobody to blame but themselves though, with that ramshackle hencoop. You build solid and you're safe.

Outside again, he looked up at the sky. There was a moon behind the clouds. It lit them enough so he could see their tattered shapes riding the wind like waves in a storm. Then he went to the back gate and checked to make sure the bars were all in place. Beyond the bar-way, the old logging road ran up along the edge of the woods. To the left of the road stood his apple trees. Under the dark, stocky shapes the snow gleamed white and smooth in the reflected light of the moon. Must be clearing, he thought. He looked at the sky again. But the moon was still behind the clouds.

He looked again at the shimmering brightness under the apple trees. Sun does that sometimes, he told himself. You stand in shadow and you see it bright on the next hill. Funny though. He set the lantern down to get the light away from his eyes. It looked even brighter now—almost like fox-fire. He looked at the more distant fields. But it wasn't anywhere else. Funny, he told himself again. Then he went back to the house.

In the kitchen his daughter-in-law was standing over a tea-kettle that was simmering on the stove. His son, George, in his undershirt, was washing his face at the sink.

"Everything OK, Pa?" his son asked.

"Clearin' a bit, I guess."

George's wife took the kettle off the stove. "Cup of tea before you go to bed?"

But Foss didn't hear her. Without answering, he clumped upstairs, full of a vague feeling that something wasn't right. His wife was already asleep. He went to the window as he undressed and looked out, even though he knew he couldn't see the orchard from the window. Then he climbed into bed gently, so as not to wake the woman beside him, and lay on his back trying to think what it was that wasn't right.

He was half asleep when it came to him. "Natalie," he said aloud. "I know what it was."

"What was?" she mumbled.

"Moon in the orchard . . . apple trees didn't have no shadows."

"Go to sleep, Willis," she said.

"How's Cruickshank going to like us barging in on him at this hour?" David asked as they sped through the dark towards the Westover corner. The snow was gone from the road, and the wet blacktop made a sticky sound under the wheels.

"Oh, I suppose he'd throw us out if he could. But we're two against one." Heron was a little tight, and he whistled softly as he drove. "You know, Dave-boy, whatever Karen told you about her father, she's not giving you a bill of goods. If she told you something, she has reason to believe it."

"But why would she believe something about her father that wasn't true, Dwight?"

"I don't know. Maybe it is true. Maybe I'm wrong. Maybe his snow crystals are just something he imagined. Who'd know better than his daughter. I know he gets thinking pretty far ahead of himself with his experiments. And he can be an awfully self-important son-of-a-bitch when he wants to be. You've got to know him. Maybe you'll think differently about him after tonight. That's why I wanted you to come up." He drove in silence for a while.

"Something's bothering Karen, Dave," he said finally. "And you know what my guess is. I think she believes that, accidentally at least, her father really did have something to do with this Cainfield mess. She feels kind of sick about it and is trying to cover for him. If what she thinks is true, she especially doesn't want you finding it out."

"Never thought of it that way. You may be right. She said something else tonight. Said he once told her he had discovered the secret of life."

"Wouldn't put it past him—to say something like that, I mean. But you know, for all his big talk, Nathan is really a good man with a test tube. A few years back he discovered a way of checking malignant tumors in rabbits that stood the medical profession on its ear. They haven't got around to trying it on humans yet. But they may be a long way towards a cure for cancer when they do."

He swung left at the Westover corner. "You know you've got to show me how to get to this place. As I told you, long as I've known Nathan, I've never been here."

"Hope I can find it in the dark. It's just a narrow dirt road off to the right, about two miles up, I think." They drove in silence then, both watching the right-hand side of the road. "That's it," David said finally. "I remember the big boulder right by the entrance." He turned to Dwight suddenly. "I thought you didn't know where it was." He had the distinct impression Dwight had started to slow the car down before he had spoken.

"I didn't. If I slowed down it was because you said two miles, and we've been two miles."

"I didn't know it was two miles. I only guessed!"

"Good guess then." Under the glare of the headlights, the snow still clung to the dirt road in patches. In between, the deep wheel ruts were soft mud, and Dwight's light convertible bounced and wavered as it crawled forward in second, and once or twice in first. Once in a while a light gust of wind sent a shower of wet snow tumbling from the trees overhead onto the windshield.

As they rounded the last curve before the turnaround in front of the old mill, David saw a pinpoint of light through the trees.

"Well, he's still up anyway," he said.

"Who, the professor? How do you know?"

"I saw the light." They pulled into the turnaround and stopped close enough so that the headlights lighted the stone-colored walls of the mill.

"If you saw a light, you saw more than I do." David could see that the mill was completely dark.

"I could swear I saw a light," he said. "Maybe he's just gone to bed."

They got out of the car and stood looking at the mill. Dwight turned the headlights out, plunging everything except the luminous sky where some moonlight came through the ragged clouds, into almost total darkness. But still no light showed in the mill. There was no sound but the sound of the millrace and the little brook that followed the road.

"Turn the lights on again," David said. Dwight fumbled at the dashboard and once again two harsh circles of orange light struck the wall of the mill, and a dim light reached to the woods on either side of the circle. David went up and knocked loudly several times on the door. Then he listened. There was still no sound from inside the mill, and no light. Finally Dwight came up behind him.

"Don't think you'll get any answer, Dave. His car isn't here."

David turned around. "What? You sure?" Enough of the headlight beam was reflected off the wall of the mill so he could see to the furthest edge of the circle. There was no car.

"But Dwight, he was here this noon. And he hadn't come home by quarter of nine. I know because I was with Karen at her house till then. And I distinctly saw a light as we came up the drive just now."

"You sure it wasn't just the headlight reflecting on one of the windows? His car sure as hell didn't drive itself out of here."

"I suppose it could have been. But it didn't look like it. Let's take a look at the tire tracks. That might tell us something. It stopped snowing late this afternoon." Dwight got a flashlight out of the car and they went to where David remembered seeing the car earlier in the day. "Should be about here," he said, pointing while Dwight directed the flashlight beam. The surface of the snow was uneven, and pockmarked with snow-droppings from the trees overhead.

But there were no tire marks where the car had been. There were no tire marks anywhere in the circle except those made by Dwight's car, and no footprints except their own.

17 . . .

"Dwight, that car was here this noon. I saw it. Karen saw it. There's less than two inches of snow on the ground here. That isn't enough to have covered up the tracks." They stood facing each other in the darkness, Dwight's flashlight making a small bright spot on the snow between them.

"You sure we turned up the right road—sure this is the right place?" Dwight switched his flashlight towards the mill and followed its outline with the narrow beam.

"There couldn't be another building in the whole state of New Hampshire that looked like this one," David said. "This is the place we came to all right. No doubt about that."

"There is also no doubt that, if the car was here as you say this noon—and I'm not doubting you about that—the professor, or somebody, has driven it away in the meantime. And in that case there are bound to be tracks, or at least traces of tracks, somewhere in this driveway."

"Well, there don't seem to be."

"You know, Dave-boy," Dwight said after they had gone over the ground again, "we're wasting time. If there aren't any tracks it's because the snow did fill them in, or there's some other perfectly logical explanation, though damned if I can think what it would be at the moment. The important thing is that the car's gone and so is Cruickshank. It would be pretty far-fetched to figure anyone else drove the car out of here."

"Unless, of course, the professor's still in there and something's happened to him."

"In which case his car would still be here—unless, of course, someone came up here on foot, knocked him over the head and stole his car. Crazy as things have been around here the last couple of days, I don't think there's any reason to think that happened." Dwight switched his flashlight back to the dark windows of the mill that reflected broken fragments of light from the headlights of the car.

"Maybe we ought to see if there isn't some way of getting in," David suggested, "just to make sure everything's all right. I could swear I saw a light as we came up the drive."

"Maybe you're right," Dwight said without much enthusiasm. "Front door locked?"

"Seemed to be. Got one of those things in the car you take hubcaps off with?"

"Think so. What are you going to do with that?"

"See if we can get a window open."

Dwight found the requisite tool in the trunk compartment after some minutes of groping with the flashlight. "Dave-boy, I don't like this," he said as he lowered the lid again. "For all we know, Nathan's safe at home in bed by this time." He played his flashlight on the dark building again.

"But the chances are he isn't. You wouldn't be getting nervous, would you, Dwight?"

"Frankly, yes. How about you?"

"Me too," David said. "If that was a light I saw, it didn't turn itself out."

"Comforting thought." Dwight gratefully yielded the flashlight to David as the latter approached the first of the two windows in the one-story part of the mill. David tried both windows, first by hand and then wedging Dwight's cold chisel under the frame and prying upward. But both were locked. There was a metal cellar door down a flight of stone steps. But that was locked too.

"No luck, eh?" Dwight said as David gave up at last. There was a note of relief in his voice.

"Might be something around the side," David said. There was only one way to go around, because the two-story side of the mill rose straight out of the pond. As Dwight followed uneasily several paces behind, David squeezed his way between the wall and the wet leaves of a thicket of alder bushes that slapped his face in the darkness above the narrow beam of the light. There was no window in the side wall—only a stone chimney. He tried to remember from that noon whether he had seen a door or windows at the back of the kitchen, but couldn't. "You wait out in front, Dwight," he called, remembering Heron's massive bulk. "If I can get in through the back, I'll open the door."

As he reached the back corner of the wall he turned the flashlight on what lay ahead of him. The beam glinted on dark water between clumps of alder and withering snake-grass. As he came around the back of the mill, his feet sank to the ankles in chilling ooze, still unfrozen under a sprinkling of wet snow. In the darkness ahead of him there was a sudden quick spattering noise, followed by a splash and then silence again. For a moment David froze, his flashlight pointed in the direction of the sound, his heart pounding in his ears. Then he reminded himself sheepishly that it was probably only a muskrat, and turned his attention to the wall. There was a window in it and this one was open.

Once he had pried it up a little with the cold chisel, it slid up easily and he crawled through it head first into the darkness inside, the flashlight still clutched firmly in one hand. Once inside he picked himself up quickly and ran the light around the room and across the floor.

In the dim, darting light the kitchen looked just the same as it had earlier that day. The coffee pot was still on the stove. The professor's leather briefcase still lay open on top of the rumpled blankets that covered the army cot. And the ashes in the fireplace still glowed. Somewhere the loud ticking of an alarm clock accented the stillness of the room.

David found the light cord and switched on the overhead light. Then he turned the spring lock on the front door and let Dwight in. Dwight stepped quickly into the lighted room. "I still don't like this, Dave," he said. "Nathan would be pretty sore if he knew what we were doing."

"I'm beginning to feel kind of foolish about it myself," David said. "Everything looks all right." They glanced about the room for a few moments in silence. "He must have left just after Karen and I did," David went on. "That's probably why the car tracks don't show. It hadn't been snowing long, and not much would have collected on the ground here in the woods yet."

"Well, if he did, somebody's been here since." David turned to Dwight who was standing by the stove.

"How do you know?"

"Stove isn't on. But the coffee pot's still hot." David came over and felt the pot. It was almost too hot to touch. The two looked at each other for a moment. "Dwight," David said, almost in a whisper, "that *was* a light I saw. There *is* somebody here." Perhaps it was some special quality in the silence; more likely, though, he thought, it was his own overwrought imagination. But David had felt since he climbed in through the window that he was not alone in the building. He felt it almost overpoweringly now—a feeling that somewhere in the dark corners of the unfinished part of the building beyond the kitchen, somebody was waiting and listening —somebody who had no business being there.

He told himself he was acting like a child who turns on the light quickly in a darkened room for fear some nameless something will pounce on him before he can reach the switch. But the feeling persisted.

With Dwight behind him, he went to the door at one end of the kitchen, behind which, he remembered, there was a sort of airway with a door opening onto the stairs leading down to the basement laboratory. He opened the door quickly, as if expecting to catch someone listening behind it.

The smaller room was dark, and smelled of decaying wood. By the light of the flash he could see the cobwebbed, hand-hewn beams and damp-stained planking of the walls. Against the far wall a flight of steps without guardrail ran up to a dark hole in the ceiling. Turning the flashlight beam into the hole, he could see part of one wall of the room above —bare and damp-stained like the wall below. Under the steps was an unpainted, heavy wooden door with a Yale lock. The wood of the door was new, and stood out in sharp contrast to the dusty, rust-colored planking of the wall on either side. David remembered this as the door to the laboratory. He tried it and found it locked.

"Don't think anyone could get in there," he whispered. "I remember the lab has a couple of cellar windows. But they looked too small for anyone to get through. And there doesn't seem to be any way of opening the cellar door from the outside. Don't think the professor would leave an extra key to this door around."

"What about up there?" Dwight nodded at the stairs.

"Doesn't look as though anyone had been up here for a long time," David said, turning the flashlight on the dusty treads. "Wait a minute!" He held the flashlight closer. "Someone has been up here. You can see the marks in the dust. I'm going up." He felt his heart pounding again as he started up the railingless steps, keeping close to the wall, and holding the light ready as if it were a gun.

"Nothing here, Dwight," he called down a moment later. The room under the gable roof of the mill was completely bare and empty except for a porcelain tray in the middle of the floor which had a little water in it. Flashing his light about the room from the head of the stairs, David noticed there were disturbances in the dust near the tray as if someone had been walking around it. In one place a rectangular, dust-free space indicated where another object about the size of the tray had rested on the floor for some time. A curious mouldy smell hung in the stale air. David was wondering why the smell was vaguely familiar when he heard a sudden cry from Dwight at the foot of the stairs.

"Jesus! Dave, quick!" At the foot of the stairs, David found Dwight with the flashlight beam. He had backed away from something near the far wall of the airway, and was standing, rigid with fright, staring down at something in the darkness near the floor. "There's someone there—on the floor . . ." Dwight's voice was faint and hardly recognizable.

David turned his flashlight where Dwight indicated. Then he almost laughed aloud with relief. A large burlap sack, about the thickness of a man's body, lay across the floor near the far wall.

Dwight still had trouble with his voice. "Christ, Dave, I stumbled on it. I thought it was Nathan!" David bent down over the sack. One end of it was open and he felt inside. Then he stood up.

"Rock salt," he said. "Must have to use it on the drive in winter." David realized that his knees were shaking. "Don't scare me like that again," he said, clapping a hand on Dwight's shoulder.

"Sorry, Dave. Think I need a drink. Let's get out of here and do what we should have done in the first place—go back to town, call Karen and see if her father's come home."

Half an hour later David called from Dwight's house. It was a long time before he heard Karen's sleepy voice on the other end of the line.

"No, Dave, Dad won't be home until tomorrow night or Tuesday morning. Why?"

"Karen . . . we were just up at the lab, Dwight and I . . ."

"At this time of night?"

"Well, never mind why right now. Karen, your father isn't there. His car's gone, I . . ."

"Oh, darling, is that what you're worried about? You should have called me before you went up there. Dad sent me a wire from White River Junction just after you left. He had to go to New York unexpectedly. See you tomorrow, Dave?"

"Yes, darling, I'll call you."

"White River Junction's just across the river," was Dwight's comment when David told him. "Funny he'd wire instead of phoning."

A lot of things were funny, David thought later as he lay in bed in his own room, watching the shadows of branches move back and forth across the street lamp outside his window. Ever since afternoon a lot of things had been going on that didn't make sense. But he was too tired to try to piece them together. There had been a light in the mill as they drove up—he was sure of that still. And yet there couldn't have been because the professor was on his way to New York. For the same reason the coffee pot couldn't have been hot, but it was. There was something else he ought to remember . . . about the mouldy smell in the upstairs room of the mill.

He remembered now why it was familiar—where he had smelled it before. It was in the Gorts' hencoop that morning as they had stood looking down at the remains of the eighteen dead hens.

18 ...

MONDAY MORNING dawned clear and crisply cool. Under the bright sun the snow vanished almost magically from the paved roads, leaving only patches of wet. And by midmorning acres of green had begun to show through the thin snow covering of the fields. Blue asters bloomed still along the fences, and yellow and red leaves dropped quietly from birches and maples that were still in the full glory of their autumn colors.

Outwardly the town of Cainfield appeared to have forgotten the events of the day before. The snow was gone from the sunlit streets. Children bicycled off to school, housewives began to assemble the week's laundry and shopkeepers opened their stores as if it were just another Monday.

But there was a black banner headline in the Lebanon *Valley Times*, the nearest thing Cainfield had to its own daily newspaper. The Manchester *Globe-Democrat*, which served the same purpose for the whole of New Hampshire, had a smaller front-page story. And even the Boston papers had stories on the inside pages.

The *Valley Times*, being the most nearly local paper, had the completest story. "COUPLE FOUND DEAD IN CAINFIELD SNOW" the headline ran, an inch high and running the full width of the front page. "Mystery Surrounds Death of Pair in Freak Storm."

CAINFIELD, Monday, Oct. 9—Death struck mysteriously on Barker Mountain Rd. near here early yesterday afternoon, claiming as its victims a 23-year old Cainfield man and his woman companion.

The bodies were discovered about 2:30 P.M. during the height of yesterday's snowstorm by Gordon L. Hewitt of Framingham, Mass., a passing motorist who found them lying in the snow in front of their stalled car about a quarter of a mile west of the junction of Routes 12 and 32, commonly known as Westover Corner.

The man was identified as Geoffrion LeBeau of this town. Papers in her purse tentatively identified the woman as Polly Carpenter, 22, of 7 Elm St., White River Junction, Vt. Both Miss Carpenter and LeBeau were employes of the R. J. Pursey Manufacturing Company in White River Junction.

County Sheriff Edward T. McEwen stated yesterday evening that the cause of the deaths remained to be determined. Neither he, nor Cainfield Police Chief Osbert L. Carmichael, nor the State Police who have been called in on the case would comment on possible causes beyond stating that violence was not suspected and that the deaths were apparently not the result of a motor accident.

Investigation of the deaths was continuing, Chief Carmichael told the press last night, and further developments could be expected in the "near future."

The *Valley Times* story went on to say that Arman LeBeau, the dead man's father, was in a state of collapse after viewing the remains of his son at the Cainfield hospital morgue and consequently unavailable for comment. It added that Polly Carpenter's roommate in White River Junction was apparently out of town for the weekend, but would be asked to make positive identification of the girl upon her return.

In another section of both the *Valley Times* and the Manchester *Globe-Democrat,* a brief obituary noted that John Bailey, 60, "a resident of Cainfield for 35 years" had "died suddenly at his home." And on the back page of the *Valley Times* it was briefly noted that eighteen plymouth rock hens belonging to Ephraim Gort of Cainfield had frozen to death in the unseasonable cold.

The facts were impersonal and separate still, because in Cainfield, as in any other town, even sudden death is not so unusual. But the facts fell on the ears of Cainfield like seeds on rich earth.

Mrs. Loren Tibbetts, Gothic-faced wife of the Tibbetts of Tibbetts and Latch, Cainfield's biggest real estate agency, stood waiting for Mr. Haskell to finish wrapping her groceries. "Terrible thing happened up at Barker Mountain road, wasn't it?" she said.

"Yes, 'twas." Mr. Haskell looked up at her from under the rim of the ancient sailer-straw hat that habitually covered his bald crown during working hours.

"Not fitting to speak ill of the dead," Mrs. Tibbetts said, "But I always said that Duke LeBeau would come to no good end."

"Had his faults like most of us, I guess," Mr. Haskell said, rubbing his hands on his stained white apron.

"Well, he and that girl certainly weren't up to any good. Tell me the car was just full of beer cans—and on a Sunday too."

"Well, Mrs. Tibbetts, I don't imagine the beer cans and whatever they was up to had much to do with it. Way I heard it . . ." he tilted the rim of his hat back and paused for dramatic effect ". . . somethin' got 'em."

"Something got them?" Mrs. Tibbetts felt a pleasurable tingle of antic-ipation. "What on earth do you mean?"

"Jes' what I say. Somethin' got 'em. Talkin' to Special Officer Jim Par-ker. 'Course he didn't like to say much. Sort of give me the impression though the two of 'em wasn't very pretty to look at when whatever it was got through with them. All chewed-up like."

"Good heavens!" Mrs. Tibbetts' eyes brightened. "You mean some wild animal, or . . ."

"Don't guess they know what it was did it . . . else they'd have told the papers about it. 'Course I don't know for sure myself. Jim Parker wa'n't exactly in a position to say much."

"I understand, of course." Mrs. Tibbetts flashed uneven teeth in a brief smile. "What you told me is quite safe with me."

When Mrs. Tibbetts left Haskell's store she was armed with a good deal more than a bag of groceries.

"Too bad about your plymouth rocks, Eph," Gene Kell said as he stuck the nozzle of the hose into the gas tank of Ephraim Gort's pick-up. "Saw it in the papers. How come they froze on you? Snow and all, didn't seem as though it could have been that cold."

"Froze? Christ almighty, Gene, them hens didn't freeze!" Gort stood glumly watching Kell, his hands thrust deep in his pockets. "Some son of a bitch down at the vet's must of give the papers that story."

"Figured something like that. Understand you had the police up there."

"Sure as hell did. That's when they found old Bailey—went down to his place afterwards to see if his hens was OK. Gene, Goddam it, somethin' et them hens of mine—leastwise tried to. Wa'n't like anything I ever seen before." In considerable detail, spiced with eloquent profanity, Gort described how he had found his chickens. When he had finished Kell put the hose nozzle back on its rack on the pump without saying anything. Then he picked up an oily rag and began to wipe his hands on it thoughtfully.

"Eph," he said finally, "I got a feeling we're in for trouble around here —big trouble. I'm not saying what I heard or where I heard it. But you go ask Chief Carmichael what the real story is on what happened to Duke LeBeau and that girl up on Barker Mountain road yesterday afternoon . . ."

By early afternoon every seat at the counter of Wendell's Grill was taken. Gene Kell pounded his beer glass on the wet linoleum. "I tell you, it's the same Goddam thing!" he was saying. "Duke LeBeau and the girl and Gorts' chickens. And I'll lay you ten to one you go up to Lavelle's Funeral Home and get Jake to let you take a look at what's left of Bailey you'd find it wasn't no heart attack."

"Carmichael and McEwen know a lot more than they're letting on, if you ask me," someone further down the counter said.

"Wasn't no human being did it," Kell went on. "Wasn't no animal either—from the sound of it."

"What did Duke's old man say?" somebody asked. "They must have called him in to identify his own son."

"Hell, he was in the tank last night. Don't imagine he's sobered up enough yet to know what he saw if he did."

"Saw McEwen, Carmichael and the state police messing around up there along Barker Mountain road this morning," someone else said. "Heard someone say McEwen had brought a Geiger counter over from the college."

"A what?"

"Geiger counter. What they measure atomic radiation with."

"Jesus Christ, what in hell they want that for?" another voice chimed in.

"Might be the best damn idea anybody's had yet," Kell said, shoving his empty beer glass at the girl behind the counter who was taking in the conversation in increasingly wide-eyed silence. "You can't tell me that H-bomb they set off out in the Pacific last week couldn't 'a' had something to do with all the Goddam snow this time of year."

"Maybe you got something, Gene," the man next to him said, his mouth full of egg sandwich. Kell leaned forward, the better to reach his audience all the way down the counter.

"Sure, maybe I got something," he said. "You guys remember that boatload of Jap fishermen out in the Pacific some time back. Some sort of ashes, looked like snow, fell on 'em after one of the bombs went off —burned the hell out of 'em. Some of 'em died 'fore they got back to port." He paused for effect. "You're Goddam right maybe I got something . . . !"

There was a long silence at the counter, punctuated by the clink of several beer glasses being set down.

"Jesus," somebody said at last, "you suppose that's why they ain't told us nothing?"

19 . . .

By TEN O'CLOCK Monday morning the last of what little snow had fallen in Westover had already gone. The sun streamed warmly through the wide window of the office of the *Westover Leader*. David, Gloria Heron and Mrs. Bigelow had gathered around the desk where Dwight sat, a pile of newspapers spread in front of him.

"They didn't get nearly as excited about it as I thought they would," David said, looking over Dwight's shoulder at the front page of the Lebanon *Valley Times*.

"I almost wish they'd run a complete picture spread with all the gory details rather than that," Dwight said. "It's what's left out of the story that's going to stand Cainfield on its ear."

"I'd like to know when somebody's going to get around to telling me what they left out," Gloria said petulantly. "Trying to get the details out of Karen and David last night was like trying to get juice out of a stone. And you're just as bad, Dwight Heron!" She leaned back sulkily in her chair and lit a cigarette. "But don't mind me, anybody. I only work here."

Dwight sighed as he looked down at the papers. " 'The repetition in a woman's ear would murder as it fell'," he quoted, then added "Shakespeare." He looked up at her then and smiled. "Wouldn't want you to get bad dreams, honey."

"Oh, hogwash!" Gloria declared. "I didn't hear Karen screaming in the night last night. Don't think I don't know why you're keeping your poor, long-suffering wife in the dark about what happened! I know what goes on in that ugly little mind of yours. You just think if you told me the details everybody in Westover would know all about it by lunchtime."

"Well, wouldn't they, my sweet?"

"That's beside the point," Gloria said.

"I'm sure I wouldn't want to hear any more about it," Mrs. Bigelow put in. "From what Mrs. Carson told me at the A & P this morning . . ."

"Of course you know," Gloria went on, "if you aren't going to tell *me* everything *you* know about all this, I'm not going to tell *you* everything *I* know."

"Oh, what now?" Dwight looked at her over his pipe as he lighted it, his eyes twinkling.

"You'll just have to find out for yourself." Gloria rose and went over to her own desk. "You amateur gumshoes can waste the morning batting the breeze. I've got my club column to get out."

"Good idea, honey," Dwight said. "Like to get that set up early. God knows what's going to come up between now and Tuesday night."

David watched Gloria spin a piece of paper into her typewriter and stare at it a few moments in silent concentration. Finally she looked up and stared in exasperation at the others who were still gathered around Dwight's desk. "Dwight Heron," she said, "I don't believe you want to know what I found out!"

"Soon's you want to tell me, honey."

"Dwight," she came over again and stood looking down at him, twisting her hands in front of her, "I don't think this is anything to joke about. Sheriff McEwen came over early this morning and talked to Dr. Nicolls, who's in charge of the physics lab at Grafton. He and Nicolls went back over to Cainfield with a—with a Geiger counter."

"With a Geiger counter!" Dwight sat up straight in his chair. "Glo, where did you hear that?"

"Mrs. Nicolls told me."

"You sure it was a Geiger counter she said?"

"Dr. Nicolls' wife ought to know what a Geiger counter is." Fright crept into her eyes. "Dwight, is there any reason to believe . . . ?"

"Honey, nobody knows what to believe and what not to believe about this." He turned to David. "My God, Dave, why didn't we think of that!"

"I don't like to think of it even now," David said. He looked at Gloria. "You mean they think the deaths were caused by radioactivity of some sort?"

"Honestly, Dave, I don't know what they think. I told you all I heard."

"Have they come back yet?" Dwight asked her.

"Don't know that either."

"What's the Nicolls' phone number?" Dwight asked and reached for the phone book without even waiting for anyone to answer.

"I certainly hope they don't find those poor people were killed by anything like that," Mrs. Bigelow said calmly. "Because if they were, then the two of you who were over there are probably shooting radioactivity all over this office right now." David felt suddenly as if the inside of his body had been flooded with ice water. He and Dwight looked at each other, the full significance of her suggestion dawning slowly.

"Oh, God! Karen was there too." David started for the other phone.

"Dave! Take it easy!" Dwight called after him. "We don't know anything like that's happened yet!" Then, regaining his customary composure, he added, "Go ahead and call her if you want to. But don't go off the deep end, and don't say anything about Geiger counters. For all we know somebody in Cainfield just lost their Goddam wrist watch in the snow." Dwight had picked up the phone. He bent over it now and began to speak in a low voice. David couldn't quite hear what he was saying. Then he hung up and looked at David, his hand still resting on the phone. "Mrs. Nicolls says they aren't back yet. She just called the Grafton lab. Says she doesn't know what the Geiger counter was for. We'd better go over to Cainfield and find out what's up."

"Then I'll have to call Karen," David said. "I was supposed to have lunch with her."

"We aren't bringing her along this time, Dave."

"You're damned right we're not!" David said. He called Briggs' photo shop.

"Hi," Karen's voice said. "I was going to call you pretty soon if you didn't."

"Everything all right?"

"Yes, Dave. Everything's all right."

"You don't sound as if everything were all right, darling."

"Dave . . . we are having lunch, aren't we? There's something I've got to tell you."

"Darling, I'm afraid it may have to wait till later. I have to go to Cainfield with Dwight right now."

"Oh, Dave! Can't you meet him there later? I've got to see you! This is terribly important! It's about Dad and everything."

"Is something wrong, Karen? Can you tell me over the phone?"

"No, I can't, and I can't get away till twelve. Please, Dave!"

"All right. Twelve o'clock at Kelsey's."

"Could we make it the Inn? Do you mind? We could talk better there . . . OK? Thanks, Dave. See you then."

"But Karen, is . . . ?" But she had already hung up. David explained briefly to Dwight, who nodded.

"That may be important too," he said. "Come by the Barker Mountain road after lunch, and if you don't see my car or any of the police there, we'll probably be down at the Cainfield station. No, you're not coming either, Glo." He caught his wife's expectant look. "One radioactive member of the family is enough. Besides somebody's got to stick around and put out the Goddam paper."

When Dwight had gone, all three settled down at their desks in silence. David looked at the clock on the wall. It was twenty past eleven. He picked up a sheaf of notes from the Westover High School sports correspondent on Saturday's football game with Dixon High. But he found he was unable to concentrate. He kept hearing the note of urgency in Karen's voice on the phone. He realized that for a moment he had even forgotten about the business of the Geiger counter.

"Dave-boy," Gloria said after a few moments, "you're not accomplishing anything over there. Neither am I. How about going to Kelsey's for a coffee? You've got time before you meet Karen." She turned to Mrs. Bigelow. "Helen? You join us?"

Mrs. Bigelow smiled and shook her head. "Somebody's got to put out the G. D. paper." Then she blushed a little at what she had said.

In Kelsey's Gloria and David took their coffee to the table nearest the window overlooking the sunlit street. "I hope you don't think I know as little about what's been going on as Dwight thinks I do," she said. "Dwight's just awfully worried about all this because he's afraid Karen's father, who of course is an old friend of his, may get himself involved."

"Everybody seems to be afraid Karen's father is going to get himself involved," David said. "Karen too."

"Yes, I know what Karen's going through, the poor kid. She told me a good deal about it last night before you came. Dwight would have conniptions if he knew what she told me."

"What did she tell you?"

"You'll find out from Karen soon enough, I guess. That's probably why she wants to have lunch with you so urgently. But I'll tell you one thing—Professor Cruickshank is involved right up to the ears in something the good Lord never intended mortal man to get involved in. And

I don't think it's his fault either—not a sweet guy like him . . ." She broke off suddenly. "Hey, isn't that Karen?"

David followed her glance. It was Karen. She was walking along the far side of the street in the direction of the Inn, apparently engaged in earnest conversation with a short, dark-haired man in khaki slacks and a leather jacket. "Who's that with her?" he asked.

"That's Dr. Nicolls," Gloria said. "Our Geiger counter man. He must have just got back."

"Dr. Nicolls!" David rose, almost upsetting his half-empty coffee cup. "I'd better get over to the Inn."

"Easy does it, Dave." Gloria smiled at him. "Won't help Karen or anybody else for you to get all wound up about this. Sit down and finish your coffee. You've got time. It isn't twelve yet."

David smiled sheepishly and sat down again on the edge of his chair. He peered out the window again. But Karen and the man with her were no longer in sight. "Don't worry, Dave," Gloria said. "She'll be there. And, as for her father—whatever has happened, he knows what he's doing. And he's got Dr. Nicolls to help him. They work together sometimes, you know."

"No, I didn't know," David said. "They work together at the lab up on the mountain?" David found himself wondering if it could have been Dr. Nicolls who had turned out the light and heated the coffee pot the night before.

"I couldn't tell you that," she said. "But I don't think he ever brings anyone up there—oh, Dwight's been up a few times, I guess, but . . ."

"Dwight has?" David stared at her. "But he told me . . ." David checked himself, feeling more confused than ever. "Look, I'd better go along, Gloria . . . Thanks for telling me what you did." He reached in his pocket.

"On me this time," she said. "Good luck."

As David came up to the door of the Inn, a large white Colonial building facing the Grafton campus, the short dark man in the leather jacket who was Dr. Nicolls came out the door hurriedly and passed him on the sidewalk. David hesitated, wanting to stop him and ask him about the Geiger counter in Cainfield. But he felt suddenly foolish, realizing what he really wanted to ask him most was what he had been talking to Karen about, and hurried up the steps into the Inn instead.

Karen was standing in the plush-carpeted lobby, looking at a window display of souvenirs. She was wearing a skirt and sweater the color of cream of tomato soup and a string of tiny pearls, and looked cool, neat and preoccupied as she turned and recognized him.

"Didn't keep you waiting, did I?" he asked.

"No, Dave." She managed a smile for him. But behind it her face was serious.

In the dining-room, an enormous room with square white wooden pillars and heavy white cloths on the tables, he reached across the table for her hand. "You've got troubles, darling," he said. "I was worried about you on the phone this morning."

"Sorry if I worried you, Dave." She squeezed his hand momentarily and looked at him earnestly as if she were going to speak, but remained silent.

"Saw you on the street a few minutes ago with—Dr. Nicolls, wasn't it? Did he say how everything turned out in Cainfield?" She had looked up at him with a sudden start as he mentioned Nicolls' name.

"No," she said. "He didn't say. He just said he'd been there. That's all . . ."

David looked at her. She kept her eyes lowered as if avoiding his gaze. "Darling," he said, "you had something you had to tell me this morning —something awfully important—about your father."

She looked up at him then, her eyes for a moment beseeching, her mouth opened as if struggling for words. Then she looked down again. "I did, Dave," she said softly. "I mean I do. But, Dave, something's come up since then. I can't tell you now. I'm sorry."

David looked up to see the waitress standing by the table. He ordered two martinis. When she had gone, he reached over and took Karen's hand again. "Karen, darling, don't you think you'd better? Whatever it is, it's tying you up in knots." She only pulled her hand out from under his and didn't answer. He found himself beginning to be angry.

"Karen, what is all this? You've been trying to tell me something about your father for a long time now. And each time you talk all around it in circles and never get to it. And this morning Dwight wanted me to go with him to Cainfield on something pretty important, and I told him I couldn't because you had something more important to tell me at lunch. And now you say you can't tell me."

She looked at him, the beginnings of tears in her eyes. "David, please believe me. Please don't be angry with me! I do have something to tell you, and I will tell you. But something happened after you phoned, and I can't tell you now."

"Did what happened have something to do with Dr. Nicolls just now?"

"Oh, David, what does it matter who it had something to do with! Won't you try and understand? Can't you trust me?"

"I'm afraid you're the one who doesn't trust me, Karen."

"That's not true, David, and you know it!"

David tried to keep the anger out of his voice. "Karen, you ask me to come here because you have to tell me something important, and then you don't. And last night you told me a lot of things about your father that, well—it wasn't entirely true what you told me, was it? You didn't tell me what you told Gloria before I came."

Now anger was kindling in Karen's eyes. "May I ask what business it is of yours, David, what I told Gloria before you came? Gloria's been the nearest thing I've had to a mother for most of my life. Three days ago I didn't know you from Adam. And now you think you own me. You think I have to tell you everything. Well, for your information, Mr. Storm, there are certain things that are none of your damn business!"

With a quizzical glance at first one and then the other, the waitress set down the martinis and discreetly withdrew.

"Take it easy, Karen," David said. "I didn't mean that to sound the way it did. But some terrible things have happened, and we're all in this together now. A lot of things have happened between us in the last couple of days, too—or I thought they had. And, Karen, three people have been killed in Cainfield, and God knows, that may be only the beginning . . ."

"And you certainly haven't been very subtle about who you think's responsible for killing them, have you?"

"Karen! I never said I blamed your father."

"No, but you think it! That's what you *think*, isn't it?" She rose abruptly from the table and looked down at him, tears in her eyes again. "Well, go on back to your paper and do your thinking there!"

"Karen, for God's sake!" David rose and came towards her. With a sob she hurried past him and out of the room and was gone. He stared after her for a moment until he realized that several other diners in the room were watching him with amused interest. Then, with trembling fingers, he reached in his pocket to pay for the untouched martinis.

20 . . .

AFTER HIS HURRIED and embarrassed departure from the Inn, David went straight to the parking space behind the *Leader* office, got in his car and headed for Cainfield. He drove scarcely conscious of the familiar road that hurtled past him as the speedometer needle wavered up to fifty-five, the most the ancient Chevrolet could do. The scene with Karen had left him numb and full of a vague, disturbing sense of loss. He could not have said whether he was angrier with Karen, or with himself for acting like a damned fool. Or maybe he was angry with Karen because he had been a damned fool.

Karen had been right. Whatever the problem was about her father, it wasn't any of his damned business. After all, he had only known her two days. As an editor of a weekly newspaper that didn't have a deadline until Tuesday night, even his connection with the strange things that were going on in Cainfield was a pretty tenuous one. Yes, he had kissed Karen impulsively while they were washing the dishes two nights ago. And last night he had told her he loved her. Could you fall in love with a girl in two days? Or did you feel that way just because you wanted to feel that way—and because maybe Karen wanted to feel that way too, for her own reasons? At any rate, the first disagreement to come along had torn the whole thing apart like a cobweb.

One thing he was sure of anyway: Karen's father did have something to do with what had happened in Cainfield. After all Gloria had confirmed his hunch about that. And if Karen had had the guts to tell him what she had apparently told Gloria, she'd have had to admit she suspected him too—or perhaps more than suspected him.

But if Professor Cruickshank was responsible in any way for what had happened in Cainfield, how was he responsible? What could he have done? What could he have got involved in that could have elicited from the totally unsuperstitious Gloria a reference to things the good Lord never intended for mortal man?

He smiled wryly as he found himself wondering if the effects of black magic were detectable with a Geiger counter.

Well, there came a time when you just had to stop worrying whether things made sense or not—when you just had to go and do what you had to.

Right now all he had to do was find Dwight. There would be time enough later to blame himself for letting Karen walk out of the dining-room feeling the way she did.

He found Dwight's car parked behind Carmichael's cruiser at the approximate spot where Duke LeBeau and Polly Carpenter had been found. But there was no sign of occupants. David parked his car behind the other two and got out. There was no snow left in the road. But there were footprints in the half-dry mud. There were also footprints where the snow remained in the field that separated the road from the slopes of Barker Mountain—footprints and something else. David stared for a moment at the close-cropped, still-green pasture that stretched almost flat for a quarter of a mile to the edge of the woods before he realized the significance of what he saw.

Except for small patches, not more than a few feet square, most of the field was already bare of snow. But starting from where he stood at the edge of the road, an unbroken ribbon of white stretched in a long arc all the way across the field to the edge of the woods. It was perhaps eight or ten yards wide where it began at his feet and seemed to grow wider as it progressed across the field.

He knew all at once that he was looking at the visible track of whatever it was that up until now had left no mark except upon the bodies of men and animals and the bark of young trees that stood in the way of its passing. For a moment he felt the ice water within him again. But at least now the enemy had revealed his position. And already the others were following the trail. He saw the several sets of footprints with green grass showing through them that marred the smoothness of the white ribbon.

The snow in the track was apparently harmless, then, and not more than a half an inch deep. Ignoring the fact he had forgotten to change his shoes for walking in the snow and wore only low cut moccasin-type loafers, he set out to follow the footprints.

There were at least four or five sets, criss-crossing the widening strip of snow and sometimes veering off onto the grass. They followed the snow across a stone wall, and a narrow brook, neither of which seemed to have altered the shape or course of the mysterious track. The track finally ended in the unmelted snow that still covered the ground where the wooded slope began. And it was here that David found Dwight, McEwen, Carmichael, and Special Officer Parker. They had seen him coming and were standing in a group at the edge of the woods awaiting his approach.

"You're early, Dave. Didn't expect you so soon," Dwight said. "Everything all right with Karen?" Dwight looked cold and uncomfortable in wet shoes and trenchcoat with turned up collar, his pipe clenched grimly between his teeth.

"Tell you later," David said. "What's happening here?"

"Dr. Nicolls from Grafton was over earlier with a Geiger counter," McEwen said. "Went over the ground with it all the way from Gorts' past Bailey's place up to here. Not a Goddam peep out of it. So that's another idea shot to hell."

"You notice the strip out in the field, Dave, where the snow hadn't melted?" Dwight asked.

"How could I help noticing?"

"Looks like we owe you an apology for not believing your theory about the snow, Dave," Carmichael said.

"I suppose it could be coincidence," David said, "just happened to melt that way."

"Not likely though," McEwen put in. "We followed that damned track in the snow pretty much all the way from Gorts' henhouse. Only a few feet wide to begin with, and got bigger as it went along. Widened out pretty sudden at the place where we found Bailey."

"But nothing registered on the Geiger counter anywhere?"

"Not a thing. Even tried it on that." McEwen pointed to something that lay in the snow not far from where they stood. David saw with a start that it was the emaciated, half-skeletonized body of a rabbit.

"God! Where did you find that?"

"Just a few paces up in the woods," Officer Parker said.

"Seems like it's headed up onto the mountain," McEwen said. "Bark eaten off a lot of the little trees, just like down along the road there. Doesn't seem to bother the bigger trees with thick bark much."

"How far up in the woods did you go?" David asked.

"No further than where we found the rabbit. Snow looked a little deeper than it ought to be beyond there. No sense taking chances. You know," he added, "I'm mighty glad that Geiger counter didn't turn up anything. But I'm not sure we're any better off because it didn't. At least if this damned snow had turned out to be radioactive, we'd have known what we were up against."

"So where do we stand now?" Dwight asked, beginning to look increasingly uncomfortable. "Where do we go from here?"

"We're on Willis Foss' land here," Carmichael said. "His farm's just around the point of woods over there, right up against the side of the mountain. Think we better stop by and warn him while we're here about going up in the woods."

"Maybe you're right," McEwen said. "Anyone else live along the edge of the mountain here?"

"No, he's the only one."

"What do you want to do about the rabbit, Chief?" Parker wanted to know.

"Better take it down to the car. We'll meet you there."

"Hell with the rabbit!" McEwen said. "My guess is we'll find plenty more like that before we're through." McEwen spoke as if he were thinking about something else. David noticed that his face looked grey and drawn as if he hadn't slept for a long time.

"OK, leave it then, and come on with us. We ought to know by this time what Doc Callan would say about it anyhow." Surprisingly enough, David thought, Carmichael looked much more his normal, ruddy-faced self than he had the day before. Perhaps, he thought, Carmichael, being a man who knew his limits, had simply decided the events of the last few days were beyond his comprehension. He would fulfill the functions of his office to the best of his ability in this or any other emergency. But he was apparently not a man to lose sleep about the aspects of a problem that continued to baffle his uncomplicated mind.

Parker gratefully turned his back on the remains of the rabbit, and the five of them set out along the edge of the woods, keeping to the field where the snow had melted and the grass was already drying in the bright sun. On the way David told Dwight about his quarrel with Karen.

"Wouldn't worry about it," Dwight said. "She's just upset. So are you. Hell, we all are. Suppose you haven't had any lunch either then? Things always look worse when you haven't had any lunch." He managed a not very convincing smile.

They came to a fence corner with a bar-way where the edge of the woods turned back at right angles towards the mountain, giving way to Foss' apple orchard. Beyond the orchard Barker Mountain, still bright with its autumn colors, rose gently almost up to its final crest, a dark, spruce-covered bluff, the bald crown of which still gleamed with snow.

When they had climbed the gate, David saw McEwen stop under one of the apple trees and kick something with his feet. In a moment all five had gathered around him.

The thin covering of snow still lay evenly under the trees with no patches of green. The longer grass that thrust up through it was strangely wilted and streaked with black. What McEwen had been kicking was one of a number of small brown pulpy objects that lay under the trees, each perched on its own little mesa of snow that raised it slightly above the level of the snow around it. David picked up one of the objects by the stem that still protruded from it. It had once been an apple. There was nothing left of it now but a withered nucleus of shredded pulp with a stem attached.

"You're taking an awful chance picking that up, Dave-boy," Dwight said after they had all looked at it in silence for a moment.

"Don't think so," David said. "If it's running true to form, we don't have to worry as long as the snow's as shallow as this."

"Already come and gone, it looks like," McEwen said. He and Carmichael had bent down under the nearest tree and were studying the base of the trunk. "You can see where it's been at the tree," McEwen went on. Between the flaking outer segments of bark, deep cracks revealed the yellow sapwood underneath. And the younger suckling shoots, the bark of which was still smooth, were all completely girdled at the base —some for only a few inches, others for more than a foot above the ground.

"Looks like the whole orchard got it," Carmichael said as they continued on. No one else had anything to say until they reached the bar-way at the other end of the orchard that opened into Foss' barnyard. Foss met them there without surprise and with only a nod of greeting, as if he had been watching their approach.

"Little out of your way, ain't you, Carmichael?" he said, his face dour and impassive. "Most folks come by the road."

"Sorry about trespassing, Willis," Carmichael said. "Police business I'm afraid. Guess you heard we've been having some trouble."

"I guess I've heard some things. Ain't no trouble around here, though. Ain't goin' to be, what's more." Foss looked at them defiantly.

"Well, we certainly don't want you to have any trouble," McEwen told him. "That's why we're here. What happened in your orchard?"

"Ain't nothin' but windfall left out there. Crops all in two weeks gone. I guess we can take care of ourselves, Sheriff."

"Haven't noticed anything else peculiar around here, have you?" Carmichael asked.

"Ain't no trouble around here," Foss repeated.

"Willis," Carmichael went on, "you know two people were killed on the road up here yesterday afternoon—maybe a quarter of a mile from your place. We don't know what did it. We have reason to think it's something in the snow—something that's still in the snow somewhere up in the woods here."

"Don't seem very likely to me," Foss said. But his eyes looked troubled now.

"We think it is likely, Mr. Foss," McEwen said, "because we've just come through your orchard, and we know it's been there. We don't know what the hell it is, but we think the chances are it's in those woods up behind your orchard right now. And we wanted to advise you and everybody in your family to stay out of the woods for your own safety until we can find out more about it."

Foss' face continued to look troubled. "Ain't nothin' in them woods." He turned to one side and spat on the ground. "Was up the loggin' rud there good half mile this forenoon. Guess I'd seen anything there was."

"Would you mind going up there with us now and showing us where you were then?"

For a long moment Foss looked at the sheriff in doubtful silence. Then he shrugged almost imperceptibly. "Guess I did leave one of my wedges up there this forenoon where I was cuttin'. Just as easy to fetch it now as later." He swung himself over the bar-way with easy agility and joined the group. A moment later they were on their way single file up the snow-covered logging road, Foss in the lead, David and Dwight bringing up the rear.

The logging road followed the east end of the orchard for a hundred yards and then entered the woods where it climbed steeply, following a dry stream bed through a forest of birch and purple-leaved moosewood. Both road and stream bed lay at the bottom of a gully, the banks of which rose higher than a man's head on either side. David found himself watching the bases of the smaller tree trunks for signs of the telltale girdling. But he saw none. Once a grey squirrel barked on top of the bank as they passed and scuttled into the branches of an overhanging beech tree, and a pair of crows flapped lazily overhead, uttering their sharp, warning cries as the column advanced. Otherwise nothing disturbed the bright, leaf-shadowed stillness of the forest.

Then suddenly Foss, at the head of the column, stopped and raised his hand. As the others came to a stop behind him, David saw what Foss had seen.

Just ahead of them the narrow gully was choked with white mist that seemed to be rising in slow billows like smoke. As the mist rose and thinned out, its individual particles gleamed diamond-bright in the sun for a moment before they disappeared. None of the six moved or spoke. As they watched, the dazzling mist shuddered and shot upwards into the sunlight as if impelled by a gust of wind from underneath. For a moment, David could see what lay behind the mist. What he saw was a wall of sparkling snow that filled the entire gully like a miniature glacier. And the wall seemed to be in motion, its whole front cascading downwards like loose sand. Then the shining mist rose again, blotting out the walls. And this time thin streamers of the same mist drifted into the air from the top of the bank above their heads on the left, and several thin trickles of powdery snow slipped over the edge and drifted like sugar onto the yellow sand of the embankment.

"Jesus, it's after us!" It was McEwen who broke the silence, his voice cracking into a momentary falsetto of panic.

David, who stood behind him, gripped his arm and seized Dwight's with his other hand. "Let's get out of here—fast," he said.

Back at the bar-way they stood awhile, waiting to catch their breath—all eyes still on the dark archway where the logging road entered the woods as if they could still see what they had seen. McEwen had regained his composure somewhat, if not his breath. "You better stay out of those woods," he told Foss between gasps. "Can't assume responsibility if you don't."

"Lived here forty year," Foss said. "Ain't likely to let anything keep me out of my own woods." He looked up at the road and his fists clenched, his eyes became hard as grey steel. But he was visibly trembling.

21 . . .

SPECIAL OFFICER MILLER, a lanky grey-haired man who habitually wore a puckered frown that made him look as if he had been sucking on a lemon, was on duty in the Cainfield police station when they returned. He rose from the desk as he saw Carmichael, his puckered mouth grimmer than usual. "Mighty glad you're back, Chief," he said. "All hell's been breaking loose around here." He picked up a scribbled sheet of paper from the desk and read from his notes. "Reporters from the Manchester *Globe-Democrat,* the Claremont *Bugle* and the *Valley Times* been in and out all morning. Want to know what's the story on the Geiger counter. I told 'em no use coming back before three. You'd give 'em a statement then.

"Also," he went on, "Vermont state police called; said Polly Carpenter's roommate is back and ready to come over and make the identification soon's we want to fetch her. Also Mr. Bricker, the county solicitor, has been trying to get in touch with Sheriff McEwen all morning . . . Also, Chief, Don Rowley wants to see you and McEwen upstairs in the selectmen's office soon as you come in."

"Can't want to see us any worse than we want to see him," McEwen said.

"Also," Miller went on, "a man named Manning called from the Waverton. Said you wanted to see him about—about mice, he said."

"Well, you can tell Manning—" McEwen gave explicit and unprintable instructions as to what Manning could do with his mice. Then he turned to Dwight and David. "You two better come upstairs too," he said.

"You know about as much about it as we do." The four of them went up the narrow stairs at the back of the police station, and through the empty courtroom to the hallway with its glass-panelled doors where Selectman Don Rowley's office was. Rowley, a round-faced, mild-looking man with thinning hair, looked up from a stack of papers and adjusted his bifocals.

"Christ, McEwen," he demanded, "what's going on around here?" He rose from his desk and paced the floor nervously without apparently noticing the presence of the others. "It's all over town you had a Geiger counter up on Barker Mountain road and over at Gorts' this morning. And about a half an hour ago Gene Kell came in here with some of the bunch that hang out over in Wendell's Grill and said they wanted the full story on what was going on up there or there was going to be trouble.

"Look, gentlemen," he continued without giving McEwen or Carmichael a chance to speak, "I know you've got your jobs to do, and I don't suppose it's any picnic after what happened yesterday. And I've got my job to do. But I'm also Director of Civilian Defense in this town. And if you have any reason to believe these deaths yesterday were caused by any kind of radiation, then by God it's my business to know about it too—it's the whole Goddam state's business to know about it!" He took a cleaning tissue from his pocket and began to wipe his glasses.

"Geiger counter was just a hunch, Don," McEwen explained. "We didn't find anything with it. Went all the way from Gorts' past Bailey's place up to Barker Mountain with it."

"Thank God for that!" Rowley said. "But you should have got in touch with me anyway. And that brings up something else. What's all this about a tie-in between what happened yesterday afternoon and Bailey and the Gorts' chickens? Somebody started a hell of a nasty rumor about that, and the press is onto it already. I've been denying it all morning."

"It's no rumor, Don. We've just come back from up there. When you hear the rest of it, maybe you'll wish it had been atomic radiation. Least we'd know what that was." Seeing Rowley's eyes shift to Dwight and David for the first time, he explained their presence.

"Hi, Dwight," the selectman said in a suddenly subdued voice, and sank slowly back into his chair.

In detail McEwen told the story of what had happened as far as they knew. David was surprised how closely the sheriff's outline paralleled the one he had made for Dwight the evening before. Only when he came to the description of the moving snow in the gully did McEwen falter and become inarticulate, his eyes haunted again with his remembered panic.

"It seems to be able to blow up into the air in clouds like that even when there isn't any wind," David put in. "And we've pretty well established from the direction it has travelled in that it can move against the wind—as if driven by a force of its own."

Rowley wiped his glasses again and was silent for long minutes. "But how is such a thing possible?" he asked at last, more as if he were speaking to himself than to the others.

"It must be possible," Dwight said, "because it's happened and we've seen it."

"Unless . . ." Rowley still seemed to be thinking aloud. Then suddenly he looked up at the others. "Unless, of course, we're under attack and don't know it."

"Under attack? What do you mean, Don?" Carmichael asked.

"Just because it isn't atomic doesn't mean the Reds couldn't have cooked up some new kind of secret weapon—something we have no way of detecting, or guarding against."

"But how was it dropped, then?" David put in. "Somebody would have spotted strange aircraft somewhere."

"Maybe it wasn't dropped from a plane."

"And why the hell would anybody want to drop it on Cainfield?" Dwight wanted to know.

"Maybe they didn't intend it to drop on Cainfield. Might have been aimed at Boston. Or maybe it was just something they set adrift like those Jap balloons on the West Coast during the last war that just blew up anywhere they happened to land."

"Look," David said, "none of us know what this thing is, but there's no use letting our imaginations run away with us. We can't prove it isn't some sort of a Russian secret weapon. But I think it's damned unlikely. In the first place, it seems to be either the snow itself, or something in the snow. And as far as we know, it can't operate anywhere except where there's snow on the ground. It isn't likely any foreign power planning to attack this country got wind of the fact Cainfield was having a freak snowstorm this early in the fall in time to drop something into it within an hour or so. In the second place, why would they want to even if they could? Anybody attacking this country is going to have to do it by surprise and try to knock us out with the first blow. You can't tell me the Communists or anybody else are going to waste their advantage of surprise, not to mention run the risk of revealing a top secret weapon just to knock off eighteen plymouth rock hens and three local citizens."

"You may be right," Rowley said. "But this town has a well-organized civil defense set-up—one of the best in any town in the state, if I do say so. And as long as there's any possibility we've been attacked—as long as the lives of any Cainfield citizens may be in danger—we've got to go into action!" Rowley slapped the palms of his hands down on the top of the desk.

"That's fine, Don," McEwen said after a moment's silence. "But just what do you plan to do?"

The glint of determination that had momentarily kindled the selectman's eyes as he spoke faded. He took off his glasses and once more began to wipe them. "Well . . . first thing I'm going to do," he said finally, "is call up Colonel Percheron in Concord. He's head of state-wide civil defense, you know. All units in the state ought to be alerted just in case."

"Just one thing, Don," Dwight said. "We don't know much about this thing yet. If the word gets around and gets in the papers there's even a remote chance of an enemy secret weapon being involved, there's going to be hell to pay. Not only would we have Concord up here. We'd have Washington up here. And once the word got around you might start the whole damned population of Boston and every big city in New England running for the hills. And if it turned out to be a false alarm, you know where our necks would be."

Rowley nodded slowly. "What do you suggest we do, then, Dwight?"

"I suggest you call a town meeting just as quick as you can get everybody together. This afternoon if you can do it. Get the press in there and get Carmichael here and McEwen and Doc Markel up on the stand and give it to 'em straight—everything you've got. Tell 'em there isn't any danger of atomic radiation and that nobody's in danger as long as he doesn't go into the snow up on Barker Mountain. Tell the truth—that's the best way to spike rumors, I say."

"Wouldn't work, Dwight," McEwen said. "Wouldn't work unless we know what the truth is. And we don't. That way you'd have ten times as many rumors flying around as you've got now."

"That's right, Dwight," Rowley said. "Never been a town meeting called suddenly like that in the history of Cainfield. Everybody'd know we were pretty scared about something. End result would be just the same as if we alerted civil defense." Rowley had begun to regain his momentarily shattered composure. "First thing we've got to do," he went on, "is call a press conference—decide just what we want to tell them, and get Gene Kell in on it too before he stirs things up any more. Second thing is, we've got to decide what to do about the thing itself before it does any more damage. You got any plans about that, McEwen—or you, Os?"

McEwen and Carmichael looked at each other for a moment. "Only thing I think of," McEwen said, "is get a crew of men together and go up there and try to find out just what it is and how far it's spread in the woods. Don't know any way of tackling the thing itself unless we put a fire hose on it."

"From what you tell me, it would be a little dangerous taking a crew up there wouldn't it?"

"They could wear cloth around their boots," David said. "From what we've seen so far it doesn't penetrate clothing except rubber and leather."

"Think you could get any volunteers?" Rowley asked McEwen.

"Think so. Imagine Gene Kell could help us with that."

"You can count on me for one," David told him.

The press conference was set for two-thirty, and McEwen told David he would try to have a crew ready to go on the mountain by four, which would leave a good two hours for reconnoitering before dark. Then David and Dwight left in their separate cars to return to Westover. David followed Dwight's car all the way and pulled up behind it outside of the *Leader* office.

"Thought you were going to change for your expedition," Dwight said as they climbed out simultaneously.

"Want to call Karen first," said David.

"Couldn't even wait till you got home, eh? Dave, I wouldn't call her yet if I were you. Let her worry a little. After all, she was the one who walked out on you at lunch—and after telling you how urgently she had to see you. You're the one who ought to be sore at her, seems to me."

David hesitated. "Maybe you're right," he said.

"Dave, you sure you want to go on this expedition? Might be risky, you know. I don't want to have to dig you out of the snow afterwards."

David stood with his hand on the car door handle and looked at the other. "Dwight," he said, "I've got to stay with this thing till we find out what it is. It isn't so much because of what happened to those people over in Cainfield. I don't suppose honestly I'd care so much about that except as a news story. But Karen's father's mixed up in this somehow, and I've got to do what I can about it for Karen's sake. Maybe it sounds silly, after only knowing her three days—but I'm in love with Karen, Dwight, and I want to marry her . . ."

Dwight smiled. "Doesn't sound silly. Doesn't sound silly at all." He clapped a hand on David's shoulder. "Good luck, Dave-boy." Dwight's wet shoes squelched a little as he walked to the door of the office.

22 . . .

It was a few minutes before four when David got back to the Cainfield police station wearing his field jacket and army slacks with the bottoms stuffed into heavy wool socks for complete insulation. He carried another pair of heavy wool socks to pull over his shoes when they reached the snow.

McEwen and Parker, similarly equipped, were waiting with Officer Miller, who was on duty at the desk. Carmichael, McEwen said, was on his way over to White River Junction to pick up Polly Carpenter's roommate for the identification and wouldn't be going along. The press conference, he said, had gone as well as could be expected. The reporters had quickly maneuvered Rowley into permitting them to use the phrase "poisonous snow" as the probable cause of the Gort, Bailey, and Barker Mountain episodes which were now officially linked together. They agreed to quote McEwen that "the possibility that the deaths could have been caused accidentally or deliberately by atomic radiation or any other man-made chemical device or secret weapon has been definitely ruled out." But they agreed only on condition that one of their number, who would release his story to the other papers as well, be permitted to accompany the Barker Mountain crew. And John Whitcomb of the *Valley Times* had won the toss.

Gene Kell, on learning that the Geiger counter tests were negative, had readily agreed to recruit a crew of ten able-bodied men and get them and the *Valley Times* man to Barker Mountain road by four o'clock. McEwen had also called up Haugsrud, and the state police lieutenant had agreed to set up road blocks to keep the curious away from that section of Barker Mountain road while the reconnaissance was under way. "Also called up Willis Foss," McEwen told David. "Said he didn't mind us going through his woods, long as we didn't leave any gates down. But he didn't want any part of it. Guess the old bastard's scared all right. Can't blame him." He grinned sheepishly. "Guess I was myself up there."

David followed Parker and McEwen in his own car. It was quarter past four when they pulled up behind Gene Kell's truck not far from the place where the mysterious snow strip crossed the field into the woods. The strip was still there, David noticed. But in the bright sun the temperature had been above forty all afternoon. It had melted considerably and was less regular in shape now.

McEwen quickly assembled Kell's group for briefing. Most of them were dressed much as David was and had pulled either socks or flour bags over their shoes. A few carried shovels. Among the group, David recognized Ephraim Gort.

As the men gathered around him, McEwen quickly explained the situation. "We're going to move into the woods in a single line," he told them, "and I want you to keep about ten yards apart—no further than that because we don't want anyone to get separated from the others." He had them line up facing him then, with Parker at one end of the line and Kell on the other. David found himself near the center of the line next to a short, stocky, blond-haired man of about his own age, dressed in a shaggy tweed suit, who carried a clipboard under one arm. He recognized Whitcomb of the *Valley Times*.

"We don't know what the hell this thing is," McEwen was saying as he stood in front of the group, "but what we're trying to do this afternoon is track it—find out how far it's gone in the woods and how much area it's covered. If possible, we want to find out where it is now. What we're looking for is small trees with the bark chewed off around the base and any dead animals or birds that look as if they'd been part-way eaten. Anything you see like that, pass the word down the line.

"Want to warn you men," he went on, "this thing may be dangerous. If the snow gets any deeper than four inches or so where you are, stop and pass the word down. And especially, if you see any snow blowing or drifting, stop! Stop and holler! I've got a whistle here," he added. "If I blow it once, everybody stop; twice, everybody assemble around me—I'll be in the middle of the line. If I blow it three times—" he glanced significantly around the group for a moment—"everybody get the hell out of the woods and meet at the cars."

On the way across the field to the woods, David and Whitcomb introduced themselves. "How'd you rate getting in on this?" Whitcomb wanted to know. "Didn't think there were going to be any other reporters."

"I'm just covering incidentally," David said. "We don't go to press till Thursday, so I won't be getting in your hair. I just happened to be along when they found Bailey. So I guess I've sort of been in on it from the start."

"You what?" Whitcomb stared at him. "You mean you've known about all this since yesterday and been sitting on it?"

"Couldn't help it. They weren't ready to release anything. It would have just been my neck if I'd crossed them up."

"Oh, brother," Whitcomb said, "am I glad I met you! You and I have got things to talk about!" He paused in the middle of his enthusiasm and looked at David quizzically. "Or have we?" he added.

"Nothing to talk about right now," David said. "As far as facts go, I don't know anything more than you." He walked in silence for a moment, an idea beginning to turn over in his mind. Suddenly he stopped and turned to the other. "Look," he said, "I'd rather you didn't ask me to tell you about this now. It would put me on the spot, and I wouldn't be able to prove anything. But if you can be patient, I may be able to give you the real story before long—so you have it before anyone else."

"How can you do that? You know something the police don't?"

"Maybe."

"My friend, you've got yourself a deal!" Whitcomb hesitated a moment. "I know you asked me to lay off the questions for now," he went on, "but I've got to ask you one. What's behind this statement of McEwen's about atomic radiation and secret weapons? I'll take his word for it there isn't any danger of radiation. Otherwise we sure as hell wouldn't be up here. But is he really afraid the Reds may have dropped something on us?"

"As you've guessed, what he said about having conclusive evidence they didn't is a lot of crap. And for a while this morning Rowley was so convinced they had he was ready to man the barricades with his civil defense crew. No, they don't know for sure it isn't the Russians. But I do know—don't ask me why yet. So, for Christssake, play that angle down in your story!"

"Glad to know that," Whitcomb said. Then he was thoughtfully silent a moment. "You know, Storm," he said, "I appreciate you promising me an exclusive on this. But if you really know as much as you say you do about it, it seems to me you might even be able to save some lives by coming out with what you know and telling the police about it. Or aren't newspapermen supposed to have consciences? I don't know. Maybe I haven't been in the game long enough."

"Don't get me wrong," David said. "I know nothing more than McEwen does about what this thing actually is, what it can do, or how to stop it. All I know is that I think somebody else is working on it too—somebody who has a better chance of finding the answer than we do—provided he's left alone."

"Is that a hunch, or do you know?"

"Maybe it's a little of both," David said.

At the edge of the woods the group fanned out in accordance with McEwen's instructions, the sheriff establishing the middle of the line at what he estimated to be the center point of the place where the snow track across the field entered the woods. On either side of him, the others took up their positions. For the most part they moved silently, and spoke little to each other. There was no joking or horse play—not since they had seen the track in the snow, and McEwen had told them what it was. They were like a squad of soldiers, David thought, enduring the last moments of waiting before advancing on an enemy position.

McEwen gave the signal to advance, throwing his arm up and forward, and David was suddenly struck with a feeling that their whole mission was a ludicrous one. Thirteen grown men, frightened half to death and deadly serious, advancing like battle skirmishers on an empty, snow-covered hillside. It was wrong and incredible and outrageous that the snow, scarcely two inches deep, that he trampled under the ridiculous wool-sock covering of his shoes, could be anything but ordinary, harmless snow—snow that would melt in a while and find its way through the earth to one of the little feeder brooks of the Saugus River that wound through Miller's flats below Cainfield. And it wasn't anything more than ordinary snow. And yet the small trees rising out of it here had been stripped of bark. There had been two horribly ravaged human faces staring up out of the snow, and the thing that had once been a girl's clenched fist, and diamond-bright mist that could move against the wind.

For the first hundred yards the reports of stripped saplings came only from the right flank of the line where Gene Kell, on the end, followed the fence of Foss' orchard. And after the first few rods David had seen no further signs of damage from his position just left of center.

"This must be where it swung out across the orchard," McEwen said. "Imagine we'll strike the trail again as we come around back of the orchard towards where we were this noon on the logging road." He passed the word down to Kell to keep along the fence as it turned the corner.

But just then Whitcomb on David's left called out to him, "Deep snow on the left—about eight inches—getting deeper." David passed the word to McEwen and the latter blew his whistle twice. "Parker," McEwen said when the crew had assembled, "take the three men on your end and head straight uphill. Don't go into the snow more than knee deep if it gets that high. And if you see it blowing anywhere or shifting, or if anyone starts to get burned, head back down here fast. You shouldn't have any trouble up there, because I think the thing we're after headed across the orchard. But what I want you to try and find out is how big an area the deep snow covers up there and how deep it gets. Also keep an eye out for tree damage and dead game. You can find us from our trail if you're finished before we are. Fire your gun if you're in trouble."

The groups separated, David and Whitcomb now forming the left flank of the main group which continued to advance through the hundred yards of woods nearest the Foss orchard. As McEwen had anticipated, they found no more stripped saplings until they had rounded the fence corner and were approaching the logging road. Then the evidence was unmistakable. Even some of the larger trees, especially the beeches with their thin skin of smooth grey bark, were partially girdled. What had once been a bed of ferns, perhaps thirty feet long and half as wide, lay shrivelled, blackened and covered with tiny star-specks of frost. A shout from the right announced the discovery of the remains of a grey squirrel, almost entirely consumed except for hair and bones.

When they reached the logging road, McEwen halted the group again and reformed the line so it spread out westward from the crest of the gully overlooking the road. "Not more than a hundred yards ahead of here where we saw it this noon," he warned. "Look out for mist—kind of a silvery mist."

"He saw it?" Whitcomb whispered to David.

"So did I."

"Jesus! What's it like?"

"You'll know when you see it."

"Can you always see it?"

"Wish I knew," David said. They moved slowly and silently after that. The setting sun made shadows of men and trees stretch endlessly across the snow. Overhead a light wind rustled the yellow leaves of the beeches. But under the trees it was still except for the harsh cry of a bluejay coming from somewhere on the slope ahead of them.

David stepped up onto a log that blocked his path. He reached down with one hand to steady himself. But as his fingertips touched the cold of the snow he drew them back sharply, remembering he wore no gloves. Without the suddenly withdrawn support of his hand, he lost his balance and fell forward on the other side of the log. His knees, hands and face were plunged into snow that was not wet like the snow they had been walking through, but soft and powdery and more than a foot deep.

With a gasp of panic he struggled back over the log, trying simultaneously to brush the snow from his exposed hands and face as if he had fallen into a swarm of bees. "Deep snow!" he cried before he had even been able to get to his feet. Almost simultaneously the same cry went up from further down the line.

McEwen and Whitcomb had hurried to David's side. "You all right, Storm? You burned any?" McEwen asked.

"Doesn't seem so." David finished brushing himself off, feeling a little sheepish after his display of panic. "God, it was deep though!" He glanced at the other men along the line. They had all stopped and several had started moving in towards McEwen, glancing back nervously over their shoulders. Kell came up from the end of the line on the run.

"Goddamndest thing," he managed between breaths as he halted by McEwen's side. "Ravine's chuck-a-block full—must be eight feet deep in there."

"Stirring around any?" McEwen asked.

"Nope. Looks like a plain ordinary drift. But Christ! Where the hell's a drift like that come from after the kind of snow we've had?"

"Looks like it's pretty deep all over up ahead," McEwen said.

"Powder too," David pointed out. "Not like this wet stuff down here. Funny it should be so dry when it still must be several degrees above freezing."

[136]

"Well, at least it ain't bit nobody yet," Kell said. "Sure like to know how deep it is up there. Guess there's only one way to find out."

"Hold it, Gene," McEwen said, restraining Kell as the latter set one foot on the log where David had slipped. "I wouldn't go up there."

"Look, McEwen," Kell said, "there's a hell of a lot more snow on this Goddam mountain than's got any business being here. But it looks like just plain ordinary snow to me. Way you talked before we come up here, I thought we was going to see something." He leaped over the log and flicked up a handful of powdery snow. "You can't tell me this stuff's what did Bailey and Duke LeBeau in. Don't know what everybody's so Goddamned afraid of." Standing knee-deep in the snow, he turned and strode towards the slope ahead. Before he had gone ten yards the level of the snow had risen almost to the level of his pants pockets. He turned around, hands on hips and looked at the group with a mocking grin. "You see, sheriff," he said, "just snow."

"God damn it, come back here, Kell!" The sheriff had hardly finished speaking when the muffled but distinct sound of a shot came from the woods to the east. The smile vanished instantly from Kell's face, and he bounded back to join the others who stood tensely listening, their eyes expectantly turned to McEwen.

"That's Parker," McEwen said, "He's in trouble. Let's go!"

23 . . .

THEY FOUND Parker and the others standing in a group around something that was lying in the snow several hundred yards further along the slope. "What happened?" McEwen demanded, out of breath from running.

"We found him just sitting there like that," Parker said, "still alive. I had to finish him off." He pointed down at the inert form of a small spike-horn buck deer lying in the snow at his feet. The deer's legs were blackened and shrivelled, and there was a wide raw patch, like a deep burn, on its belly where the skin had been eaten through.

"Christ, we thought you'd . . . hell, I don't know what we thought!" McEwen said, looking down at the deer. Then he looked at Gene Kell. "Take a good look, Kell," he said. "Guess you can figure yourself mighty damned lucky you don't look like that buck there right this minute." Kell, white faced, turned away from what lay in the snow.

"Is that . . . is that what the others looked like?" Whitcomb asked.

"Hell," said McEwen, "that buck got away before it hardly started on him. LeBeau and the girl and Bailey didn't." He turned to Parker again. "See anything at all other than this?"

Parker shook his head. "Stripped trees," he said, "and there's deep snow all along the slope up there—Lord knows how deep. Didn't want to take a chance of going too far into it."

McEwen nodded. "Here too, eh? Looks like the whole damned mountain. Didn't see anything stirring or blowing?"

"Nope. Deep snow was powder dry, but it wasn't moving. Picked some up. Didn't burn my hand any, but it felt kind of funny."

"How so?"

Parker took off his cap and scratched his head. "Hard to say," he said. "Maybe a little dryer—maybe it didn't melt quite as quick in my hand."

"Didn't burn though?"

"Nope. Held it for quite a while."

McEwen was silent a moment. He looked up at the others, standing expectantly around him and then cut across the wooded slope to where the sky was still orange-red behind the trees. Where they stood it was already twilight. "You men head back for the truck," he told the crew. "Isn't much more we can do today. Wait for us when you get there," he told Kell. Kell, his earlier exuberance completely vanished, nodded in silence, and the men started to move down the slope, leaving Whitcomb, David, Parker and McEwen standing by the deer.

"What do you make of it, Storm?" McEwen asked.

"The deep snow?"

McEwen nodded. "It snowed like hell on the mountain yesterday—and Saturday too. Didn't snow that much though—not by a long way."

"So the—the extra snow has got to have something to do with what we're looking for."

"And yet, what gets me," McEwen went on, "it didn't hurt Kell when he walked out in it. Didn't hurt Parker here when he stuck his hand in it. And Kell says even the drift in the gully where we saw it moving yesterday wasn't doing anything—looked just like ordinary snow. That's the Goddam trouble. It all looks like just ordinary snow—except it's a little dryer than it ought to be. And then we come across this . . ." He nodded down at the dead buck.

"Don't suppose you brought anything along to take samples in?" David asked.

"Matter of fact I did. Glad you reminded me." McEwen fished a small glass jar out of his pocket. "Doc Markel's idea. Wouldn't have thought of it myself." Parker showed them where the deep snow began, only a few yards above where they had been standing. It lay still and very white in the gathering twilight. The irregular line of demarcation, where the deep powdery snow had halted its advance over the shallow, damp snow underneath was still faintly visible. Gingerly, McEwen filled the bottle half full. He had to wade several steps into the deep snow in order to be sure of a pure sample of the powder. But he held the bottle so that his bare fingers did not come in contact with the snow.

"Must be only certain times or certain places it's dangerous," David said, thinking out loud. "How do you figure it?" He turned to Whitcomb.

Whitcomb still held his clipboard, but hadn't even attempted to take notes. "You're way ahead of me," he said, shaking his head slowly. Then he went back to staring at the drifts in troubled silence.

McEwen had put the sample jar back in his pocket after carefully wiping its exterior dry with a handkerchief. He stood now looking down at the snow. "Know what I want to try?" he said. "I want us to haul what's left of that buck up here and dump it in the deep snow there. We aren't going to get a better chance to see what this thing can do with our own eyes." The others looked at him in silence. "You ask me," he said, "I don't think anything'll happen if we do. I don't think we've found what we're looking for yet. I don't think this snow here's the same stuff at all we saw in the gully yesterday. Couldn't be. Too damned much of it."

"Suppose it is, though," David said. "How do we know it hasn't spread all over the whole mountainside?"

"You fellows game to find out?" Despite the challenge in the sheriff's eyes, David knew McEwen was as scared as he was. Parker's Adam's apple was bobbing up and down, and Whitcomb stood nervously a few paces back from the group, as if trying to dissociate himself from what was being planned. He looked, David thought, as if he would like to find an excuse to go back to the truck.

"What can we lose?" David said finally.

"Our skins is all," said McEwen. With each of the four reluctantly gripping one of the withered legs, the dead buck was not heavy to carry. And the four breathed heavily more from anxiety than from the exertion required. Reaching the edge of the drift, they swung their burden back and forth a couple of times, then heaved it, with all their combined strength, into the deep snow. It dropped with a muffled thud several yards in front of them, sinking deeply into the drift. Then the four stood well back from the edge of the deep snow and waited.

The dusk had deepened so that the dead buck was only a dark indistinct shape against the motionless whiteness. David, straining his ears and eyes as the minutes dragged on, heard nothing and saw nothing to indicate any reaction in the snow around the carcass of the deer. Further up the slope where the white of snow faded into the gathering shadows under the trees, there was also nothing stirring—no breath of wind, not even the occasional chirping of small birds. "Guess I was right for once," McEwen said. "I told you it didn't look like that other snow we saw yester. . ."

It was then that it happened. David thought at first it was a trick of his eyes after staring too long and too intently at the white drifts. It looked like a faint pulse of brightness that leaped towards them across the surface of the deep snow and vanished as if the distant circular beam of a searchlight had passed over the ground, but so faint he would not have been sure it was not an illusion had he not heard McEwen's sudden exclamation.

"Storm! Did you see that?" As they watched it came again, a dim, cold flicker that spread like a ripple on water, only incredibly faster. David saw that there was a change in the snow. Less of the deer carcass was visible now. Around it small eddies of snow curled lazily like the wisps of smoke that rise from a piece of paper thrown flat on top of a fire just before it ignites.

"Oh, God, look! It's burning! The snow's burning!" Whitcomb's voice was almost hysterical as he pointed.

As they ran down the slope towards the edge of the woods, David, bringing up the rear, stopped once and turned to look back. Far behind him the slope that should have been lost in shadow under the trees was bathed in a soft light, as if the moon were shining on it.

"That was Sheriff McEwen again, wasn't it?" Natalie Foss looked at her husband over her glasses. She did not break the rhythm of her knitting as she looked up. Her husband said something that sounded like "eee-yuh" without taking his pipe out of his mouth. They were sitting in the room next to the kitchen where they always sat after supper, Natalie by the table with the lamp, and Willis in his rocking chair by the window, staring out into the darkness towards the barn. At another table, Willis's son George and his wife, Ethel, sat playing gin rummy.

"What'd he want this time?"

"Sheriff?" Willis took his pipe out of his mouth. "Didn't say exactly. Suppose he's still tryin' to find out what happened to the LeBeau boy and the girl up by the corner yesterday."

"What's he doin' in our woods then?"

"Lookin' around, I guess."

Natalie Foss stopped knitting and looked at her husband again. "Willis, you acted mighty strange this noon after you'd been up in the woods with 'em. There's somethin' goin' on up there, and you know very well what it is and just won't tell me. And after some of the stories going around about what happened to those two poor . . ."

"If a man stopped to listen to all the stories he heard in this town," Willis interrupted her, "'tisn't likely he'd have much time left over to get a day's work done."

"They were saying down at Wendell's Cafe this afternoon . . ." George began from the next table.

"You want to talk about what's happenin' up in our own woods, George Foss, you'd ought to go up there yourself first and use the eyes God gave you, 'stead of tryin' to find out about it down to Wendell's." Willis rose from his chair and looked down at his son scornfully. "There's too many tongues waggin' around this town it seems to me, and too many people listenin' to 'em. This farm and this house is built solid. I know 'cause I built it that way myself these forty years gone. There's nothin' in those woods up there a God-fearin' man or his family has call to be afraid of!"

His wife looked up in mild surprise. "Why, Willis, is there something to be afraid of, then?"

"I told you no! Even if a man should see the devil with his own eyes . . ." He trailed off, looking towards the window. "I think I'll take a look at the stock."

"I'll help you, Pa." George started to rise from his chair.

"Isn't likely I need help walking to my own barn." Willis stalked out through the kitchen, took his lantern from its hook on the wall by the door and went out.

Tonight the moon was full and bright in a clear sky. And its soft light gave a blue-silver phosphorescence to the bank of mist that lay between him and the orchard and mountainside. He stood in the yard, halfway to the barn, looking at the mist and forgetting that he had not yet lighted his lantern. A damp, cold breath of air from the direction of the mountain touched his cheeks, and he saw the shining mist roll forward with it, close to the ground as if weighted down by the warmer air of the night. He heard the cows lowing in the barn, and he understood why. Already the mist was running like smoke under the fence and barway. And just as he had, the cows could smell and feel the sudden chill in the air. Or maybe animals had a way of sensing more than that.

At first, as he saw the pale, shining delta of snow spreading under the bar-way below the mist, pure animal fear possessed him, paralyzing all thought and motion. Then the fear became anger, and the anger solidified into a single knot of purpose.

He had a shovel in his hand and was driving it into the soft snow under the bar-way and hurling shovelful after shovelful back over the fence into the whirling bright mist that was all around him like flying needles. But the snow, shimmering with its own faint brightness, flowed almost like liquid, and each time filled where he had dug.

Finally he used the shovel as a club, fighting the snow, silent, alone, and with all his strength, as he had always fought for his land.

Half an hour later, Natalie Foss began to wonder aloud why her husband hadn't come back from the barn yet. Her son, George, rose reluctantly from his gin rummy game and said he would go and see. When he opened the outside door, the sparkling mist came into the kitchen.

24 . . .

It was six-thirty and already dark when David got back to Westover. He turned directly up the street that led to the Cruickshanks' house. Karen would be alone, or perhaps Gloria would be staying with her still until her father got back.

She would be happy to see him, he thought, and sorry about the way she had acted at lunch. But she would have to tell him now whatever it was about her father she had intended to tell him. If Professor Cruickshank knew anything about what was going on on the side of Barker Mountain, it no longer mattered whether he was Karen's father or not. Did Karen know the truth? Had she known it and kept silent even then? If she knew the truth, he would make her tell him now. He would make her tell him if he had to shake it out of her.

He had stopped the car and was halfway up the steps of the green-shuttered house before he realized the windows were dark. But he had to pull the bell knob several times, hearing it chime uselessly from within the house, before he could accept the fact neither Karen nor anybody else was home.

It had never occurred to him she might not be home. And she would have left a light somewhere if she had just gone out for a short time. He sat in his car in the dark for some minutes, wondering where she could be. He realized he was actually beginning to be angry with her again for not being home.

Then the thought came to him she was very likely to be at the Herons'. Knowing she would be alone for the evening, they had probably invited her over to their house for dinner. Should have thought of that in the first place, he told himself.

He called from Kelsey's and Dwight answered the phone. "Dave-boy, where are you? Thank God you're back. I've been listening to the radio this afternoon, and I was getting worried as hell about you. How soon can you get over and tell us what happened?"

"Dwight," David said as soon as he got a chance to speak, "is Karen with you?" He tried to make his voice sound casual.

"Who, no, Dave, she isn't. Gloria called her about five-thirty to see if she'd come over and eat with us, but she wasn't home. Have you tried the house?"

"There's still nobody home."

"Well, I wouldn't worry, Dave. There are lots of places she could be. She might have gone over to White River Junction to meet her father."

"But she hasn't got the car. And besides, she said he wasn't due until morning."

"Dave, I'm sure there isn't anything to worry about. Karen's a big girl and can take care of herself. You must be dead-beat. Why don't you come over and have a drink and some supper? And if you're worried, we can make some calls from here. But my guess is, she'll probably be back by the time you get here."

"OK, Dwight. I'll be there in a little while." He put the receiver slowly back on the hook. He knew Dwight well enough to know from the sound of his voice that he was worried too.

Pulling a phone book out of the rack, he riffled through it. He ran his finger down the row three times before he found "Briggs, Burgess W., photog" with a residence number. Briggs informed him in a clipped English accent that Miss Cruickshank had not come to work that afternoon, and that he hadn't the slightest idea where she was, since she hadn't taken the trouble to inform him of her intended absence. David hung up while he was still talking. His whole body felt as if it were made of lead.

"Is Dr. Nicolls there please?" She had been with Dr. Nicolls that noon. There was a slight hope she might have told him something. A better chance that Dr. Nicolls had told her something—something that had upset her so at lunch.

"Who's calling, please?" It was a female voice on the other end of the line. David gave his name. "This is Mrs. Nicolls, Mr. Storm. I'm afraid my husband had to leave rather unexpectedly after lunch today, and I doubt very much if he'll be back before morning. Is there any message?"

David's heart sank. "It's rather urgent," he said. "Do you know Karen Cruickshank?"

"Why, yes of course. We know Karen and her father very well."

"You haven't seen her by any chance?"

"No . . . not this afternoon."

"You don't happen to know where she is?"

"No, Mr. Storm. Is there some reason why I should?"

"Well, you see, she was talking with your husband this noon—something about her father's experiments, and I thought perhaps . . ."

Mrs. Nicolls' voice was suddenly cool. "I'm afraid I can't help you, Mr. Storm. Sorry." He heard the click on the other end of the line.

David picked up the phone book again. But he realized he knew of no one else to call.

He sat in the phone booth a moment, trying to fight down his anxiety. There was no reason to be concerned, he told himself. She had said at lunch something had come up—obviously something that had upset her badly, or she would not have got so angry with him. Perhaps her father had called from New York. He might have wanted her to come to New York. Perhaps she had gone with Dr. Nicolls—Mrs. Nicolls had said her husband might not be back till morning. If it had been an urgent message from her father, she could easily have forgotten to notify the photo shop that she wouldn't be in.

Wherever she was, he told himself, it was her business. There was no need to worry. He would stop by her house again, just in case she had come back. Then he would go home and clean up and go to Dwight's. He realized suddenly that he was terribly tired, and his nerves were still shaky from the Barker Mountain reconnaissance.

The Cruickshanks' house was still dark when he pulled up in front of it a few minutes later. This time he went around to the side door that opened into the kitchen, just to make sure. The kitchen windows were dark too as he had known they would be. He was about to turn away when something caught his eye. He looked again and saw what it was. Behind its screen, the kitchen door stood part-way open.

He went up to the door and tried the screen. The screen was not locked. The heavy inner door with its Yale lock was open about a foot. He stared at it a moment, full of a gathering sense of foreboding. In a small New Hampshire town like Westover, people very often didn't bother to lock their doors. But they very seldom left them open unless they had just stepped out for a minute. And, if Karen had done that, she at least would have left the kitchen light on. It had been fully dark for better than half an hour. She would hardly remember to turn off the light, and then forget to shut the door.

He opened the screen and stepped a little way into the kitchen. He knocked on the open door and called out, feeling foolish as he did so. But there was still no answer. He heard nothing but the ticking of a clock in the kitchen, and somewhere, the faint sound of radio music.

He realized there was nowhere radio music could be coming from except from within the empty house. He listened again. The music was faint and tentative, blurred with static. It sounded the way a radio sounds when it has been left on for a long time and has slipped out of tuning.

Something was wrong, he knew. He stepped the rest of the way into the kitchen, groped for the light cord, and pulled it. The first thing he saw as the overhead light winked into sudden brightness was the shoulder-strap handbag Karen had carried at lunch. It lay open on the kitchen table, its contents scattered over the table top and on the floor.

Fear a tight knot inside of him now, he hurried through the pantry into the dark living-room. He could see the tiny green dial light of the cabinet radio. The low, quiet voice of an announcer came from behind the static.

"Karen!" he called again. But the silence afterwards was even more oppressive than it had been before. There was something terribly wrong about the silence—about the radio left on, the door left open, and the hastily rifled handbag. Karen should have been there, and she wasn't, or if she were there . . . Without thinking what he was doing, he found the hall light and hurried up the stairs.

When he reached the upstairs landing, he saw one of the bedroom doors was open. The light from a street lamp that shone dimly into the room beyond revealed that the room was in a state of considerable disorder. Drawers were pulled out, articles of clothing were scattered on the floor, and across the bed . . . He found the light switch inside the door frame and snapped it on. What lay across the bed were the sweater and skirt Karen had worn at lunch. Suddenly David's panic vanished, and he realized that he not only had no business to be where he was, but was acting like a damned fool. Feeling like a common burglar, he turned off the lights and hurried from the house, hesitating only to wonder whether he ought to close the door, or leave it as it was. He decided to close it.

"Get hold of yourself, Dave-boy!" he told himself in the car. Suppose, he thought, Karen or her father had walked in just then. Vainly, he told himself he had been right to be suspicious and to investigate. No damned point getting in such a state of nerves because you'd seen something on Barker Mountain you couldn't have seen! What the hell did you think, Storm? That the damned snow had got into Karen's bedroom? Angrily, he drove across town to his boarding house. He was going to need that drink at Dwight's.

Mrs. Rockwell, David's landlady, was sitting in her usual chair in the front sitting room as he came in. She lowered her copy of the *Valley Times*. "Message for you, Mr. Storm," she said, "on the mantlepiece." Her narrow, angular face disappeared behind the paper again. "Young lady left it for you this noon." David found the plain blue envelope and tore it open. "David—" he read, "Back tomorrow. Don't worry about me. Forgive me about lunch. Love—Karen." Suddenly David felt less tired.

"Did the young lady say anything?" he asked.

"No. She seemed to be in a hurry. Just told me to be sure you got the letter when you came in. Terrible thing over in Cainfield. You read about it?"

"I've heard about it," David said. Suddenly he thought he knew where Karen was. "Tell me, Mrs. Rockwell," he asked, "how was the young lady who came in dressed? Did you happen to notice?"

"Why, yes . . . Matter of fact, seems to me she was wearing old clothes. Remember in particular she had a sweater on had paint all over it. Thought at the time it was kind of funny she'd be going around like that . . ."

"Lots of funny things going on, Mrs. Rockwell. Thanks for the message." David hurried back out to his car.

He was halfway to Westover corner before he realized he had completely forgotten Dwight was expecting him and he hadn't even called. Well, it was too late now. There wasn't much doubt about it, he thought. There could only be one place Karen would be going in such a hurry in her paint-stained sweater. And if she were going to the laboratory, probably with Dr. Nicolls, it meant that her father was back from New York and was there too. That would explain everything, he thought— the sudden change in her plans at lunch, her apparently hurried departure from the house. And God knows what might be happening at the lab. They must have known what was happening on Barker Mountain to have rushed out there so quickly—and so secretly. And, if that's why they had gone, then it meant Cruickshank knew the answer to what was happening in Cainfield, or thought he did—and Karen knew it too. Perhaps she had known it as she sat opposite him at lunch—wanting to tell him, and not being able to.

His foot pressed down harder on the gas as he sped through the moonlit darkness.

A few hundred yards north of the Westover corner, the blacktop road leading north to Dixon topped a rise. And this was where anyone travelling from Westover to Cainfield got their first full view of Barker Mountain. Ordinarily, on a bright moonlight night, Barker Mountain was a long, black ridge, rising slowly towards the west until the gentle slope reached the summit knob. Then it dropped away sharply towards the valley where the Dixon road went through. In silhouette, the summit knob and the western slope looked much like the head and trunk of an elephant.

David had seen Barker Mountain from the top of this rise many times before. But this time he brought his car to a squealing stop and stared at what he saw. The higher part of the mountain's western end was bathed in a faint, pulsing, phosphorescent mist. Above the mist, the mountain's bald, snow-covered crown gleamed a pale shimmering blue, outlining the black spruces that fringed it. From it, a tattered streamer of cloud that glowed like the mist fanned out westward like gale-blown snow from an alpine cornice.

And then he saw that the phosphorescent mist itself was rising like smoke. He knew that what he saw was no fantastically improbable combination of moon, wind and mist. It was the snow on Barker Mountain—ablaze with cold, impossible fire.

25 . . .

THERE WAS STILL some snow on the narrow dirt road that followed the brook up through the woods to the old mill. And the floor of the forest on either side of the road was still an even white, faintly luminous here and there where moonlight filtered down through the birch and swamp maple leaves. But it was ordinary snow, and it gleamed only where the moon touched it. As David rounded the last bend to the turnaround, the lights of the mill winked reassuringly through the trees. Thank God! he thought. But he had known the mill would not be empty. As he pulled into the turnaround, his headlights glinted on the chromium bumper of Professor Cruickshank's car.

No sooner had he shut off the motor and lights and climbed out, than the door of the mill opened. He recognized at once the slight figure that stood silhouetted against the light from inside. "Karen!" He ran towards her.

"Dave! Oh, Dave!" Karen ran to meet him and threw her arms around him. She clung to him for a moment and then looked up at him. "You got my note and you knew where to find me!" she said.

He took her shoulders and looked down at the indistinct oval of her face. "I got your note finally," he said, "but not until you'd scared the hell out of me with your disappearing act!"

"I know. I'm sorry—especially about lunch, David."

"You ought to be."

"Am I forgiven?"

"You're safe, Karen. That's all that matters."

"I don't know whether any of us are safe, darling."

David held her at arm's length and looked at her. "Karen, what's going on up here? I guessed you were coming up here when my landlady said you were wearing old clothes. But what's happening? When did your father come back from New York?"

"He didn't go to New York, darling. He's been here all the time."

"He's what?" David stared at her.

"That's why I was so upset at lunch, Dave. Dr. Nicolls had just told me."

"But he must have been here then when Dwight and I were here last night. I don't understand. Where was he? Why did he hide on us?"

For answer Karen took his hand and pointed up over the roof of the mill. "Look, David."

Where they stood, in the middle of the turnaround, the full moon was almost directly overhead. It was so bright it seemed to give even the air a faint, pearly lustre. Atop the steep bluff that rose almost vertically behind the mill, dark spruces stood out in jet black relief. Beyond them, the sky was a deep, electric blue. Barker Mountain itself was screened by the bluff. But David could see the glittering streamers of mist drifting majestically upward and outward from the hidden summit. They seemed to rise out of the top of the bluff itself.

"I know," he said. "I saw the mountain on my way here."

"David, it's worse than anybody imagined." Karen's hand felt cold in his.

David saw that another silhouetted figure had appeared in the open door. "It's all right, Dad," Karen called out. "It's David."

Professor Cruickshank came out to meet them. "Might have known you'd turn up sooner or later," he said to David. "You had no business coming here." But there was no anger in his voice, and his grip was firm as he shook David's hand. "I don't know how you found out where we were, David, unless my daughter violated security and told you. But since you are here, we can certainly use you. We've got a bad time ahead of us." He glanced up at the bluff. "I suppose you know what that is in the sky up there." David told him what he had seen from the Dixon road.

"Yes," the professor said, "it's been fulminating since about noon. We had counted on another twenty-four hours before that happened."

"What is it, Professor?"

"If it had happened in January instead of October, it might be the end of the world. We'd better go inside. We have a lot to talk about, and it's going to be dangerous out here before long." The professor spoke in a low, calm voice, but as they came through the door into the lighted interior of the mill, David noticed how haggard he looked. He wore a dirty grey shirt with the sleeves rolled up, and a rubber laboratory apron. His face was drawn and pinched, and there were dark smudges under his eyes.

Karen, in dungarees and the paint-stained T-shirt, looked tired too. Her hair was tied back haphazardly with a piece of ribbon, her forehead and cheeks were smudged with soot, and her unmade-up lips were pale.

"This is Dr. Nicolls," Cruickshank said. "David Storm, John." David recognized the short, dark-haired man who rose from the kitchen table as the one who had been with Karen that noon.

"Heard a lot about you, Dave," Nicolls said, shaking hands with a quick, friendly smile. He was dressed much as the professor was. Though he appeared less haggard, his dark eyes looked sombre and troubled. "You've walked into a lot of trouble, in case you don't know it," he said. "But glad to have you with us."

"David got a good look on the way up," the professor said. "Whole mountain is active and fulminating." Nicolls whistled softly.

"Bad as that, is it?" he said. "Guess tonight's the night then."

Cruickshank slumped down in one of the chairs pulled up to the kitchen table and looked at David. "Dwight know you're here?" he asked. "Dwight or anybody else?"

"Not a soul. I was supposed to call Dwight and forgot."

"Probably just as well. He'd be up here and all over the place. Much as I love him, Dwight isn't much of a front line soldier." He looked down at the table top. "Frankly, David, before we go any further, I'm going to tell you I think you ought to take Karen and get the hell out of here."

Karen was getting some cans down from a shelf above the stove. "You know very well, Dad, I'm not leaving here unless you do too."

"Karen, you know John and I can't leave."

"But, Dad," she turned away from the shelf and came towards him, "you said yourself it's going to reach here before long. And what will happen then? Is there really anything you and John can do by yourselves to stop it?"

"There's nobody who can do anything to stop it except John and me, Karen. And there is nothing we can do unless we are here when it comes. If we are not here, nothing we have done so far is any use."

"I know," she said. "You told me that. But were you expecting it to become so bad so soon?"

"It doesn't make any difference, Karen. If we had a week, or even a few days it would be different. We could report what we know, and have the resources of the whole state—or the whole country for that matter— working to accomplish the same thing we are trying to do. But we don't have that much time. By the time we could get anybody to believe us, it might be too late. With real winter coming, all New England might be faced with something horrible beyond all imagining. There'd be no way to stop it then."

"You think you can stop it, Dad?"

"I believe we can stop it. Whether any of us who remain here will come out alive or not, I don't know."

Nicolls, standing beside Cruickshank, ground a cigarette slowly into the ashtray on the table and looked at David. "There is a very good chance we won't, you know." David looked at Nicolls. He wondered if Mrs. Nicolls knew.

Karen looked at David and said quietly, "I'm staying, Dave."

David smiled at her. "I wasn't going anywhere either." He turned to the professor and Nicolls. "I don't know what's happening," he said. "I don't know what I'll be good for. But since I've walked into it, you can count me in."

"Have you any idea what you're letting yourself in for?" Nicolls asked.

"No. But I expect I will before long."

Nicolls grinned. "Hope you weren't planning to sleep tonight."

David discovered Karen standing expectantly beside him, her arms crossed behind her with exaggerated pertness. Under the soot smudges, her face had brightened. "Now that you are officially hired, Mr. Storm," she said, "you can make yourself useful getting some wood for the fireplace while I get supper. Come with me and I'll show you."

David followed Karen across the moonlit turnaround to where some split logs were stacked against a tree. Then, suddenly, she was in his arms. "Oh, darling," she said. "I'm not afraid, now that you're here. I just wanted to tell you that." He tilted her chin back and looked at her.

"I'm afraid, Karen. Afraid for you."

"No," she said. "You mustn't be. Nothing is going to happen to us." She laid a hand against his cheek. "Remember what you told me last night? Snow is nothing but nice clean white stuff kids make snowballs out of. As long as we believe that, we have nothing to be afraid of."

"You believe that, Karen—and you know what it is up there?"

"Yes, I know what it is."

"Then I believe it too. I love you, Karen . . ."

She clung to his arm as they started back towards the mill. "Please don't ever stop telling me that," she said. She stopped abruptly. "Don't forget the logs, silly!" Then she ran back to the house.

"I don't have to tell you what this thing we are up against has done already," Cruickshank told David during the supper Karen had prepared from cans on the shelf. "And I am sure, after what you have seen on the mountain tonight, you can imagine what it may be capable of as it continues to increase in size. It is not only the lives of us here that may be at stake in the next hours, David. If we fail in what we have to do, not only Cainfield, but all of northern New England will be in deadly peril in a matter of days. Ultimately, the threat of horrible extinction could hang over every community in the northern hemisphere where it gets cold enough to snow." For a moment silence hung over the table.

"Do you know that?" David asked finally.

The professor nodded. "We can safely assume it from what we do know."

"But . . . what is it? How did it happen?" David looked around the table at the others. Karen's grey eyes met his a moment, and then she looked down at her plate. Dr. Nicolls was looking down at his coffee cup. Cruickshank looked at the others and then turned slowly to David.

"As you suspected yesterday noon, David," he said gently, "I am responsible."

"You . . . ?" David stared at him. "Oh, no! That can't be true . . . Whatever I said yesterday . . ."

Karen continued to look down at her plate as David turned towards her. "You know perfectly well that's not true, Dad!" she said.

"Of course it's true, my dear," he said. "You and David and Dwight all suspected I was responsible. And you were quite right. I was. No, there was no negligence, or evil intention, on my part. But that doesn't change it. It was my laboratory crystals—the ones I shot into a cloud over Dixon last week—that somehow gave birth to this monster." He put his elbows on the table and leaned forward, lowering his head between them for a moment. Then he looked up again and seemed to be staring at nothing.

"There wasn't one chance in a hundred million—and yet it happened." He picked up an aluminum salt cellar and twirled it in his fingers for a moment. "This salt cellar," he said. "It is within the bounds of possibility that due to some fantastically improbable coincidence of rhythm in the motion of its electrons, this salt cellar could collapse this instant into a heap of dust, or even explode and destroy us all. The chances of what is up on Barker Mountain creating itself out of my snow crystals was just as unlikely. And yet—it happened. And so I, and only I, am responsible." He looked at David.

"I was only looking for the truth," he said, "the truth about why the cells of our own bodies can sometimes defy all their own laws of growth and heredity, and go berserk inside of us until they destroy us. The answer to that goes far beyond medicine. We call it cancer when it happens to the cells of the body—insanity when it happens to the mind. Perhaps it is the same thing when a star a million light years away flares up suddenly and becomes what we call a nova. Perhaps the very life that is in us began once in a molecule of sea water as an infinitesimal revolution against the law and order of the universe.

"I don't know," he said. "But I thought if such a revolt could be caused in a limited way in a lifeless crystal—a crystal that has the same inherency of form as a living cell . . . I succeeded better than I knew."

"You mean," David said, "what's up there on the mountain is alive?"

"Something up on the mountain is alive—alive in a strange and terrible way that is like no plant or animal life on this earth."

David stared at him in horror. "Then the luminous mist I saw on the mountain—the snow that burns things—that's alive?"

"No," the professor said. "Not by itself. Imagine a giant amoeba—a shapeless mass of protoplasm jelly with a nucleus in the center. Under the influence of that nucleus, the protoplasm devours food and grows. But cut the protoplasm off from the nucleus and it becomes nothing but lifeless jelly.

"What I am trying to say is that the luminous snow on Barker Mountain is ordinary snow which has become, you might say, the protoplasm of this living thing—capable, as we have seen, of devouring food and expanding. Somewhere on Barker Mountain is the controlling nucleus —the living thing itself. We know that this living thing, whatever it is, has the power of possessing ordinary snow and making it part of itself. And we know that, once under the influence of this nucleus, whatever it is, any snow in the world can become part of the living thing itself—capable of motion and growth, and driven by an insatiable hunger."

There was a long silence at the table. "Now do you understand," the professor said at length, "why we had to go to such apparently ridiculous lengths to keep secret our preparations for the destruction of this thing?"

"No, Professor, I don't," David said. He rose from the table and stood looking down at him. "If what you say is true, what right have you or any of us to keep it secret when whatever is up there may be killing people right now—when, if your calculations are correct, all New England is going to be in danger in the next few days? My God! The whole country ought to know about it so something could be done! What are we sitting here waiting for?"

"Sit down, David," the professor said gently. "Multiply your own excitement just now by several million and you'll have your answer. People in Cainfield are undoubtedly near enough to panic now, just from what has happened already and the display of fireworks on the mountain tonight. Can you imagine what would happen in Cainfield—and throughout the state if the truth were known?" Somewhat mollified, David sat down again.

"Frontal assault is, of course, the first thing that comes to mind in dealing with a thing like this," the professor went on. "Do something—anything! Attack it and destroy it—in this case attack it with fire or water. Something to melt the snow. I'm sure by this time they have already thought of that on the other side of the mountain.

"But it isn't that easy, David. This thing was small at first. So small that, from what Karen tells me, a little boy may well have packed it into his snowball. In fact, I think we can be quite certain the snowball that struck the Gorts' henhouse contained the nucleus. We could have destroyed it then with a few buckets of hot water, or a blowtorch. We could have destroyed it at any time up until it reached the mountain.

"But on the mountain the environment was perfect for it. The forest sheltered it from the sun and kept a vast expanse of snow from melting so quickly. The trees, and also the animals in the forest supplied it with nourishment. What it has grown into now we can only surmise from the impressive nature of its visible effects. To destroy it now, we would have to melt every drop of snow on Barker Mountain—and we could not be sure we had destroyed it even then."

"So what do we do?" David asked.

"We must wait for it to come to us here where we can guard ourselves against the effect of the snow around it."

"But how can we be sure it will come to us here?"

"That's what John and I have been working on since yesterday. We have developed a very simple instrument which we believe will guide it directly to us. It was mostly John's idea. He will explain it to you later. Our first problem now is that of placing the instrument where it will do the most good. And, because of our location here, the only logical place is on top of the bluff behind us."

"On top of the bluff?" David looked at him incredulously. "How are you going to get it up there?"

"One of us is just going to have to climb up and put it there," Nicolls said. "Unfortunately we didn't have the instrument ready in time to do it while it was still daylight."

"But what about the snow, Dad?" Karen asked.

"I told you earlier, my dear, whoever goes up is going to have to take a chance on that. Fortunately, I think we may still have a few hours before it will be dangerous up there."

"I should think," David said, "it would be bad enough getting up there in the dark even without the snow to worry about."

"It's not so bad if you go up the other side of the pond," the professor said, rising from the table. "I was up there this afternoon. I know the way." Karen rose too.

"Dad, *you're* not going!"

"Karen, we've been over all this before. One of us has to go, and we haven't much time left to argue about it."

"I think I should go, Nathan," Nicolls said. "After all, it was my idea to put it up there." He turned to Karen. "It really doesn't matter which of us goes," he said. "This is no more dangerous than what we're all going to be faced with before the night's over."

"I think I'm the logical candidate," David said. "After all, you two know what has to be done when this thing gets here. I don't. So that makes me the most expendable."

"Oh, stop acting like children!" Karen cried suddenly. "If one of you has to go, one of you has to go!" She went over to the kitchen sideboard and came back with the ends of three matches protruding from her clenched fist. "Let's decide and get it over with. One of these matches has no head." She held out her fist towards Nicolls. Nicolls looked at Cruickshank, who nodded. Then they both looked at David.

"All right with me," David said. The match Nicolls drew had a head. So did Cruickshank's. Karen looked as though she were on the verge of tears as she came up to David. "Oh, David . . ." she said. He took the headless match from her hand and touched her cheek lightly.

"Remember what you said outside just now, darling?" She bit her lip and nodded. Then suddenly she turned from him, sank down in a chair and covered her face with her hands. Her shoulders shook with silent crying.

26 . . .

Professor Cruickshank stayed with Karen while David went down to the laboratory with Dr. Nicolls. "The thing we've worked out is really quite simple," Nicolls explained. "Just a matter of small electric currents." On top of the center work table in the laboratory, David saw a large metal box with dials that looked somewhat like a radio, except that a small light bulb protruded from the top. Near it on the table lay several coils of wire and two smaller instruments. One of them looked a little like a microphone, and the other was a small metal box with what looked like a miniature television aerial protruding from it.

Nicolls went on with his explanation. "As you may know," he said, "this thing we're after activates the snow around it by means of a series of impulse waves that act like nerve impulses." David nodded. He remembered the pulsing flashes of blue light he had seen in the snow that afternoon on the other side of the mountain.

"We can't exactly explain the origin of these impulse waves, of course," Nicolls went on. "But we do know that the motivating factor is a small repeated charge of negative electricity which we have been able to measure." He smiled. "I was able to do that at one point this morning while Sheriff McEwen and I were ostensibly going over the ground with a Geiger counter.

"So, what we plan to do is to place this small instrument up on the bluff where, before long, it will come in contact with the activated snow." He picked up the small box with the special attachment. "We also place this receiving device up there," he pointed to the microphone-like instrument, "and attach them both by wire to our potentiometer here." He indicated the large radio-like box. "I won't burden you with the technical names of the small instruments, since we adapted some standard equipment from the Grafton lab especially for the purpose. Enough to say that one of the instruments will record the impulse waves on the potentiometer. The frequency of the light flashes from this bulb and the direction of the compass needle beside it will tell us how far away our nucleus is and the direction from which it is approaching. Through the other instrument, we will transmit electrical impulses back to the activated snow which are of exactly the same intensity and frequency as the impulses received from it. Our impulses, however, will be positive. And we believe that sooner or later the nucleus will be attracted to the source of the disturbance."

"You believe?"

"It's our only hope. If it doesn't come . . ." Nicolls shrugged.

"And if it does come?"

"We have plans for that too. We'll cross that bridge when we come to it."

"So what you want me to do is to plant these two instruments on the bluff and string a wire from each."

"That's right. You'd better string one going up and one going down. It'll be easier, and you won't have to carry both coils all the way up. But it isn't far." Nicolls put a hand on David's shoulder. "You don't have to do this, you know. I was planning to."

David grinned more confidently than he felt. "We're all in this together. Just hope you have a good flashlight."

A few minutes later they had all gathered in the turnaround in front of the mill. "Looks safe still," Cruickshank said as they looked up at the bluff. The moon was still bright, and to David the sky looked about the same as it had before. The streamers of mist were rising from behind the bluff. But it was hard to say from how far behind.

"Got everything?" Nicolls asked. David had one coil of wire and the knapsack containing the instruments slung from his shoulder, and he carried the second coil. A large flashlight was hooked into his belt. "It feels like it," he said. He felt for the knife and wire clippers in his pocket.

"We'll be down here with a light," Cruickshank said. "We can hear you if you call out. Best way up is across the brook and up the ridge on the other side of the pond. It's less than two hundred yards to the top. When you get there, you'll find some bare rock with a pretty good view of the top of the mountain. That's the best place to set up." He gripped David's hand. "I didn't intend for you to go, David. But perhaps you have a better chance of making it in the dark than either John or I. Good luck!"

Nicolls took one end of the coil of wire David carried, and David paid out slack as he backed up towards the laboratory door. "OK," Nicolls called finally from the door. David felt Karen beside him.

"Sorry I acted like a goop just now," she said. "Wish I could go with you and carry something. Be careful, darling!" He took her in his arms, and then was on his way down the gravelly bank to the brook, the beam of his flashlight bobbing in the underbrush ahead.

On the other side of the brook, the bank rose steeply. He stopped every few yards to pay out slack in the wire, then hooked the coil over his elbow and used both hands in climbing, keeping the flashlight hooked into his belt. At first he was climbing through thick underbrush over rough, stony ground that was almost devoid of snow because of the thick cover. With his flashlight on, he could see nothing ahead or around him but a jungle of leaves. When he turned it off he was wrapped in damp, earth-smelling total darkness. There was no way of maintaining direction except to keep going up. He stopped to rest finally and called out as loud as he could. He heard several shouts in answer, including Karen's. They came from surprisingly close below him, he thought. He had felt as if he were hundreds of feet above them by now. "OK!" he shouted back, and started climbing again.

He had not gone much further when he came out into moonlight that seemed bright as day after the darkness in the undergrowth. He was moving now through close-growing spruces, not more than ten or twelve feet high. The ground between them was choked with lichen, moss, and hip-high blueberry bushes still clotted with patches and fragments of wet snow. Overhead between the trees, he could see the sky now—enough of it to see the streamers of mist, scudding like low clouds above the crest of the slope ahead of him.

He paused to unwind some more slack wire, and then continued climbing, bearing to the left in order to keep as close to the ledge where he could maintain contact with the mill below as possible. He waved the beam of his light above the pointed tops of the spruces to the left, then turned it away. In a moment he saw the flicker of an answering beam on the tips of the furthest branches, and heard again the answering shouts from below. They sounded much further away this time.

His coil of wire was three-quarters gone, and he realized he must be almost at the top of the bluff. It had looked further than it was to the top from below, because the spruces on top of the bluff that had looked full-sized trees at a distance were actually only dwarfs.

He continued to climb and noticed that the slope began to lessen. The spruces were smaller now. Beyond their wind-twisted tops, the rising blue-silver mist pulsed and flickered coldly. From where he stood the tattered fragments of bright cloud seemed to ride so close above him, he imagined he could almost see the separate shimmering particles. A light wind stirred in the trees, and he felt it, cold against his cheek—cold and stinging, as if it carried particles of ice.

Then he came out of the trees onto a wide, almost level expanse of moon-flooded rock, blown bare of snow by the wind. He had reached the top of the bluff.

He had come out of the trees facing in the direction of the mill below, so that all he saw in the first moment was the moonlit ledge of rock and the well of darkness beyond it. Then he turned towards Barker Mountain. For a moment he could neither move nor believe what he saw.

Only the topmost peak of Barker Mountain, glacially blue-white, rose into the dark sky above the sea of fiery mist. The mist had advanced across the saddle between the mountain and the bluff to within less than a hundred yards of where he stood. The forward wall of the mist flickered blue and green, as if there were fire within it, and advance tendrils puffed and spurted towards him, then spread and slithered over the moonlit rock, like fingers of an exploring hand, before they faded.

Occasionally the mist eddied, revealing the wall of bright snow advancing behind it. David gasped at the height of the wall. There couldn't be that much snow! Not on the whole mountain!

But there was a job to do . . . His breath coming in audible gasps, and his hands shaking with the urgency of near panic, he unslung the knapsack and got out the instruments. Then he twisted the end of the double wire he had carried up the mountain twice around a small spruce growing out of a chink in the rock, and located the terminals of one of the instruments with his flashlight. His fingers felt like blocks of wood as he fastened the peeled ends of the wire under the brass knobs. When the ends were fast, he wrenched the other coil of wire from his shoulder and looked up at the mist. A gust of it caught him full in the face, burning like red hot sand.

For a moment he lowered his head, not daring to open his eyes. When he opened them again, he saw that advance streamers of mist were already flowing around him, following the grass-grown fissure lines in the smooth rock. In the light of his flashlight it looked like whitish smoke. In the dark, it gleamed silver-blue. Above him the heatless flames flashed and rose with majestic slowness, until the moon was dimmed behind their pale sickly radiance. The air around him was full of sibilant whispers, and a rising wind tugged at him in gusts full of hot needles.

Somehow he found the end of the unused coil of wire and wound it around the same small tree. This time it seemed to take even longer to fix the wire ends to the terminals. But it was finally done. As he rose to get his bearings for the dash down the slope into the trees, he had a last fleeting look at the scene before him. The peak of Barker Mountain was lost in the blaze of mist now. And down the dark slope on the far side of the bluff on which he stood, a bright cataract was hurtling downward through the trees like molten lava, glittering clouds rising in its wake.

Seizing the coil of wire, he plunged down the slope into the trees, floundering and falling as he fought his way through the resilient tangle of blueberry bushes. In a few moments he had left the pale, unearthly light of the mist-covered bluff behind him, and was down amongst the trees in real darkness again. His heart pounded furiously against his ribs and his breath came painfully, but he dared not stop even here except to pay out slack in the wire. He flashed his light into the tops of the trees and tried to signal by shouting. But he had no breath for more than a hoarse croak. He thought he heard answering cries from below. But at the same time there was another sound—an ominous rumbling and crackling from the slope above him.

He scarcely remembered how he made his way down the rest of the slope except that it was mostly by sliding and falling. Somehow he managed to cling to the light and to the coil of wire, letting it yank itself out of his hand loop by loop as he descended. It wasn't until he scrambled up the bank from the stream onto the level wet snow of the turnaround that he became conscious again of the rumbling sound he had heard on the slope. For a moment it rose to an earth-shaking roar, mixed with an ominous splintering sound. Then it ceased altogether.

Looking back, David saw that the entire slope down which he had just come was screened in silver smoke.

Then someone had gripped his shoulder reassuringly and taken the wire from him. Karen's arm was around his waist, and he was walking between her and her father towards the open, lighted doorway of the mill.

27...

DAVID LEANED back in the kitchen's one armchair, sipping gratefully at a small tumbler of whisky. Karen knelt by the chair, watching him solicitously. Her father stood behind her.

"You sure you're all right, Dave?" she asked him. He nodded. His whole body ached, his limbs smarted in dozens of places from deep scratches, and his face, where the mist had brushed it, felt as if it had been sandpapered. But he was still miraculously in one piece, and the whisky felt warm and comfortable inside of him.

"That was a close thing, Dave," Cruickshank said. "We thought we'd lost you when that avalanche started. You did a fine job. That took a lot of guts. Don't think John or I could have made it under the circumstances."

David smiled. "Hope the avalanche didn't get the wire."

"Don't think so," Cruickshank said. "Slide was further over on the slope. If it hadn't been we never would have seen you again. But we'll know in a minute. John's downstairs connecting up your wires now. What is the situation up there, Dave? Pretty bad?" David told him as best he could.

"I wouldn't guess how high that wall of snow is," he said. "But it's unbelievable."

Cruickshank nodded. "Won't be long before it's over the ledge, I guess. Looks as though the nucleus may be headed our way anyhow—even without our apparatus to guide it. Avalanched around both ends of the bluff already. We'll be trapped in here in another hour or so if my guess is right. How do you feel, Dave?"

"Ready for whatever's coming, I guess."

"You deserve a rest. But I don't think any of us is going to get much for a while." He laid a hand on Karen's head. "Karen, we've got to go down to the laboratory for a few minutes. Will you take care of things up here? Check the door and windows to make sure they're tight; get candles and kerosene lamps and first aid kits together where we can get them easily, and see that the gas is turned off in the stove. You know where the main valve is, around in back?" She nodded.

"I'll heat up some more coffee before I turn the stove off," she said, "and I'll see what I can get on the radio." Karen looked pale and tired. David caught her hand as he rose to follow the professor downstairs.

"OK?" he asked.

"OK," she said, "and I'm glad you are." She gave him a quick smile and went over to the sink, picking up dishes from the table on the way.

Under the mercury vapor lights of the laboratory, Dr. Nicolls was studying the potentiometer. "Nice going, Dave," he said. "Your connections seem to be fine. But you must have got out of there by the skin of your teeth. We're getting blips already." David noticed that the light on top of the potentiometer was winking at intervals.

"What does that mean?" he asked.

"It means the instruments you planted up there are in contact with the snow already—probably covered with it." He turned to Cruickshank. "Needle points directly at the bluff. Can't tell how far the receiver up there is from the source of current. But we're getting a blip every ten seconds. If it speeds up we'll know it's getting closer."

"Our signal getting up there all right?" Cruickshank asked.

"It's registering on the dial," Nicolls said. David watched the two dials on the face of the potentiometer. One of them jumped every ten seconds, synchronizing with the flashing light. The other jumped the same way a few seconds later.

"What happens when the thing we're waiting for reaches the instruments up there?" David wanted to know.

"While you were gone," Nicolls said, "I placed another of the current discharging devices like the one you took up the bluff just outside here on the turnaround." David saw the unattached wire hanging from one of the small windows high up in the wall. "By that time the active snow will have reached here. We'll simply connect up that wire and start sending from here instead of from the top of the bluff. . . ." Nicolls ran a hand wearily through his hair and looked up at the professor. "I wish to God we could be sure that signal of ours will do any good."

"I expect we'll know before long," Cruickshank said. "But in the meantime, I'd like to go over our plan of action. Prefer to do it while Karen's upstairs," he added. He met David's troubled look. "You see, Dave, as you may have guessed by now, we don't know how good our prospects of getting out of this alive are. We're reasonably certain we can bring this nucleus here to the mill. But we can't know exactly what we are going to be in for when it comes. All we know is that we must destroy it —even if we have to destroy ourselves in the process. From what we've told you already, David, you must understand the importance of that." David nodded.

"John here accepted the risk knowingly," Cruickshank went on. "I might add, so did his wife. But it's my fault Karen is here, and consequently that you are. I had to ask John to bring her here this afternoon, David. I had to explain to her that I had not brought this thing into the world intentionally—I should have known she wouldn't leave." He sighed. "Well, that's water under the bridge. If worse comes to worst, David, I'm going to count on you to get her out. After what you did this evening, I think you could do it if anybody could. I have a feeling you will, whatever happens." He smiled and gripped David's arm.

"But enough of that. The next thing on the program, David, is a quick chemistry lesson."

"Chemistry lesson?"

"When faced with the unknown, David, one should first arm oneself with all the facts there are. This is no supernatural monster you found yourself face to face with up there on the bluff. I won't say it's flesh and blood like us, because it isn't. But it's made of the same elements we are, David, and in its own way, obeys the same laws of nature. God knows it's a thing to be feared. But we must fear it intelligently if we are to conquer it."

Cruickshank pulled a chair up to the table alongside of Nicolls and arranged some sheets of scratch paper in front of him. David sat on the edge of the table.

"I don't know how much you know about chemistry, David," the professor said, "but surely you know the chemical formula for water is H_2O—two hydrogen atoms to one of oxygen. Well, ordinary water isn't all H_2O. The hydrogen atoms combine with the oxygen atoms in three different ways actually, and all water has small amounts of what we call dihydrol—H_2O_2, and trihydrol, H_2O_3 in it. These are called heavy water, and their physical properties are a little different from ordinary H_2O. For one thing, they have a higher freezing point, and are not very stable. They tend ordinarily to break down into ordinary water and free oxygen.

"Now, just how I made my special crystals—the ones that caused all this when I used them for cloud-seeding—is a secret that, under the circumstances, is going to be buried with Dr. Nicolls and me. I doubt very much if you, as a layman, could follow us if we did try to explain it. But I did succeed in doing what I set out to do—making artificial snow crystals composed almost entirely of H_2O_2 instead of ordinary water, which were consequently less stable than the ordinary variety.

"But something unexpected happened. Certain impurities in the water vapor we used apparently had a catalytic effect on the crystals when they came in contact simultaneously with air and certain organic materials such as rubber, leather—or flesh. What the catalytic effect caused was a chemical reaction which is simple enough to write an equation for, but which simply does not take place under ordinary circumstances." As David looked over his shoulder, Cruickshank wrote on one of the pieces of scratch paper in front of him:

$$N_2 + 2H_2O_2 \longrightarrow 2HNO_3 + H_2O$$

"What that means, David, is that our heavy water crystals showed a tendency to combine with free nitrogen in the air to form pure nitric acid and ordinary water. That's what accounted for the moisture affinity, and the burning effect on organic matter.

"Here in the lab, this was only an incomplete reaction which never progressed very far. But the wonder is it happened at all. You may know that one of the biggest problems of modern industrial and agricultural chemistry has been that of trying to make free nitrogen in the air combine chemically with oxygen. It just doesn't.

"There are what we call 'nitrogen fixing' bacteria in the roots of certain plants which can turn free nitrogen into the nitrates needed in the soil for plant growth. But we don't know how they do it. We can't imitate the process in the lab, any more than we can imitate the process of photosynthesis in plants—making carbohydrates out of carbon dioxide and water with sunlight as a catalyst.

"So, there is your picture, David. When, through some strange chemical accident in the upper air, which will always remain a mystery to us, these crystals of mine developed the power to complete this reaction within themselves, they became alive in a strange way. Our form of life is chemically no more than a slow, controlled combustion which uses oxygen as fuel. This form of life in the snow is a combustion too—not always so slow and controlled. The shining mists we see are actually the flames of combustion—but of a strange cold form of combustion that uses not oxygen but nitrogen for fuel! And a by-product of this combustion is the corrosive acid it used to digest its food.

"David, what I thought was crystalline twinning in my laboratory crystals was actually the beginnings of cell division. What is up there on the mountain is a negative form of life, completely hostile to our own—hostile even to itself, because it cannot exist for long without destroying the very environment which makes its existence possible.

"If we fail to destroy it now, it will destroy itself ultimately. But not, I fear, until it starves to death after having destroyed all other earthly life that it can reach."

"Blips at eight seconds," Nicolls said. "It's getting closer."

The professor nodded, then looked at David. "Well," he said, "now you know what we're up against." David felt strangely as if he had known for a long time. But it seemed a little less horrible now that it had been explained in terms of plain chemistry.

"This is our plan," Cruickshank said. "When our instruments tell us the nucleus—the source of current—is directly outside the mill, we're going to open the cellar door to the lab here and let it in." David stared at Cruickshank, feeling a cold prickling along the nape of his neck.

"My God!" he said. "Let it in here?"

Cruickshank nodded. "The door opens in and springs shut. Once there is no longer any pressure on it from outside, it will close of its own accord. That way we will have the nucleus trapped in here and cut off from its snow which should then stop fulminating and cease to be dangerous."

"But suppose it's too big to get in here? Or doesn't choose to come in the door? Does it have enough of a brain to come after us?"

"For various reasons, I think it unlikely that it will be too big. And, once it is here, I think we can count on its coming in the open door. Its evolution has been so fantastically rapid, I don't believe it has had time to develop any kind of a brain. But it obviously has enough instinct of self-preservation to seek food and shelter. Look how it travelled toward the mountain against the wind! I think it will be aware of the presence of both shelter and food here in the laboratory."

"And once it's in the laboratory—what do we do then?"

Cruickshank pointed to a fire hose hanging on the wall near the foot of the stairs. "I had that put in for emergency," he said. "The pipe connects directly with the millpond on the other side of that wall. The level of the pond is a good four feet above the floor of the lab. We simply lock the thing in here and turn on the water."

"And if that doesn't work?"

"Then we burn or blow up the mill on top of it. If the thing is trapped inside, we might be able to escape safely through the snow."

Just then there were quick steps on the stairs, and Karen burst into the lab. "Dad!" she cried. "I've just heard it on the radio . . ." She stared at them wide-eyed, unable for a moment to speak.

"What, Karen?" her father said. "What is it?"

"The Foss' farm on the other side of the mountain—where David was . . . the snow got it. Foss and his son were killed. They found them in the barnyard. House is still full of snow. The fire department's trying to melt it down with hoses and get in—they think Foss' wife and his son's wife are still in there . . . oh, it's . . ." She ran to David and clung to him. The professor and Nicolls started for the stairs.

"The newscast's over," she said. "I waited till the end. They've got all the roads around the mountain blocked off. They're sending the state guard and the governor's declaring a local emergency . . ."

"My God!" the professor said. "That's two miles away!"

"We'd better take a look and see what's happening outside," Nicolls said.

A moment later all four of them stood in the turnaround. The mist had completely screened the bluff, and David saw the moon shining wanly through the cold flames overhead, just as he had seen it earlier from the tip of the bluff. On all sides of the turnaround, the mist was rising in vigorous billows like smoke from a forest fire. A gust of it eddied towards them from the ravine where the road and brook entered the forest. And behind it, they could see the snow.

When everyone was inside again, Cruickshank closed the door and turned to face the others. "Well, we're alone with it now," he said. "It's got us surrounded. But there's no time for any of us to worry about that. I don't *think* the snow can get in here till we let it. First thing to do is to get everything moveable upstairs from the lab. Optical instruments and chemicals first," he said.

28 . . .

It was almost midnight by the time they finished transporting everything from the lab upstairs that was both worth salvaging and small enough to be moveable. Upstairs a forest of bottles and glassware filled half of one end of the kitchen floor. Downstairs, in the denuded laboratory, nothing remained on the long table but several loose sheets of scrap paper, an electric ring with coffee pot and cups, and the potentiometer with its wires leading under the metal laboratory door. On the dials, David noticed as he passed by, the needles were jumping much more rapidly now.

After they had brought up the last load and checked the lab for anything missing, Karen and David stood watching Nicolls at the potentiometer. Cruickshank came back from the tiny washroom under the stairs, rubbing a towel through his hair. He had taken off his thick glasses, and David could see the gaunt hollowness of his eyes.

"Better get some sleep, Karen," the professor said. "The cot's yours and there are plenty of blankets. There's nothing to do but wait now. You might as well rest while you can."

"You'd better get some sleep yourself, Dad!"

"John and I are going to be down here with this for a while." He laid a hand on the potentiometer. "David, I want you to stay with Karen upstairs and keep an eye on what's going on outside. I don't have to tell you not to go outside, or even open the door. Let us know if there's any change."

"Got enough coffee?" Karen asked as she and David started towards the stairs. But both Nicolls and Cruickshank were already bent over the dials and didn't hear her.

Karen walked over towards one of the windows in the kitchen. "Turn out the light, Dave," she said. He flicked the switch by the door and came over to where he saw her silhouette against the pale blue light that came through the window. For a moment they stood side by side in silence.

Outside deep, shining snow already covered the turnaround, and David could see the steady pulsing of its brightness. The glittering mist stirred and brushed silently against the window, and he was reminded again of fingers, reaching and groping.

"It's like a blizzard," Karen said softly. "It's almost beautiful. What is it, Dave? Is it really alive?"

"Your father says so. I suppose it is in a way. I don't think we'll ever know." She took his hand and squeezed it tightly. "Births, marriages and deaths and unimportant snowstorms," he said. "Remember?"

"I remember. That was only the day before yesterday."

"Karen," he said, still looking out the window, "what were you going to tell me at lunch today?"

"Nothing you don't know already by now," she said. "Am I forgiven? About lunch, I mean?" He turned towards her and kissed her for answer.

"You've known about this for some time, haven't you?" he said. "It must have been awful for you, Karen."

She walked over towards the fireplace where the coals still glowed red in the darkness. "No," she said. "I didn't know about this until Dr. Nicolls told me just before I met you at lunch. He had called up McEwen this morning and suggested trying the Geiger counter because he wanted an excuse to get a look at what was happening over there. After what he saw, he felt he had to tell me where Dad was and what he was doing. I made him bring me here. Now you know why I was so upset at lunch." David came and and stood beside her.

"But you were upset before that, Karen."

"Of course I was. Dad didn't know exactly what was going to happen till we came up here yesterday, but he had told me about his crystals before. He told me he was afraid something might happen—that he might have accidentally created some kind of life. How was I to believe even my own father when he told me things like that? I thought he was beginning to make himself sick, being up here so much by himself." She sat down on the edge of the cot, still looking into the fire.

"Last week, after Dad had been up in the plane over Dixon, I was so upset about it, I went and spilled everything to Gloria and Dwight. They thought I was imagining things—especially after Dwight went up to see Dad at the lab one night, and Dad didn't tell him anything." Perhaps, David thought, her father had told Dwight something—had told him so much he didn't dare talk about it. That might explain why he had said he had never been to the laboratory.

"Silly," Karen went on, "but I guess one of the things that bothered me most this noon was when Dr. Nicolls told me how he and Dad had engineered Dad's so-called 'trip to New York' yesterday without telling me what was really happening."

"What did really happen?"

"Oh, Dad drove his car over to Nicolls' place just after we were here. Nicolls drove him back to the foot of the road here and let him walk back to the lab. Then he parked Dad's car by the station at White River Junction and sent me the telegram signing Dad's name. It all seemed so childish and unnecessary. And yet, I suppose it wasn't.

"Oh, David," she went on, "if only I had believed Dad—if only I had dared talk to you after what happened Sunday morning—if I had told you some of the things Dad had told me—we might have been able to prevent all this. But, David, it was so horrible—how was I to think . . . how was I to know?"

"Karen, darling, it wasn't your fault! You mustn't blame yourself! How could you know? How could anyone know what was actually going to happen—even your father?"

She gripped his hands suddenly. "Oh, darling, we are going to get out of here—aren't we? We aren't going to—die like Bailey and the others?"

He held her close to him. "No, Karen."

"It's bad though, isn't it, Dave? What Dad told you downstairs?"

"We'll be safe, Karen. I won't let anything happen to us."

"Will there ever be a world again after this where kids can make snowballs? Where . . ." Her voice was muffled as she pressed her face into his thick wool shirt.

"Yes, there will be, Karen. And for us, too."

"For us?"

"For us, Karen." He spoke, looking at the coals of the fire, holding her head against his chest still, and aware of the faint piney scent of her hair. "We haven't known each other very long. As a matter of fact we haven't yet even succeeded in having a complete lunch together. I don't suppose I even know much about myself and what I'm good for—except to write about small snowstorms and things for a weekly paper. But I want to find out what I'm good for, Karen, and I'm going to. And, wherever I go from here, I want you to go with me."

"That sounds like a proposal, Mr. Storm," she said without looking up.

"It does, sort of," he said. She raised her head and looked at him, her face only a few inches from his.

"I want to be with you too, David—always."

She lay back on the cot, her face pale and luminous in the dim light of the dying fire. He sat on the edge of the cot, looking down at her. "Don't let me be afraid, David!" she whispered. He bent down to her and she clung to him tightly. And for a long time they lay very still together.

David raised his head finally, hearing a soft footstep at the other end of the kitchen. The professor was standing by one of the windows, his face close to the glass. David could see the glint of the pale light on his glasses. He stood very still, and David had the feeling he had been standing there a long time.

Karen twisted her head on the blanket pillow. "Dad?" The professor continued to look out of the window. "Thought you were asleep, Karen. It looks bad out there. . . . Trying to get in the window. . . . Gathering its forces for the attack. Where's David?"

"Right here," David said.

"Oh." The professor turned from the window finally. He came over towards them. "Everything all right?" he asked.

"Outside?" David asked. "Doesn't sound that way."

"I didn't mean outside." Cruickshank came and sat down in a chair near the cot and looked at them. David couldn't see his eyes. "It isn't outside that matters," he went on. "It's whether you're afraid inside. You two aren't afraid, are you?"

"No," David said. "Not now."

"Good. That's good."

"David says he wants to marry me," Karen said. The professor nodded slowly, showing no surprise.

"God bless you, my children," he said. "And don't ever be afraid of life. You get lost when you are. You find yourself terribly alone."

He paused to light a cigarette, tossing the match towards the fireplace. "She'll make you a good wife, David," he said finally. "She's like her mother in many ways."

"You have been lonely, haven't you, Dad?" Karen said.

The professor's face was half lighted for a moment by the glowing ash of his cigarette. "Human beings weren't ever meant to be too much alone," he said. "Let a man take himself away from the people around him, and it's like taking an outboard motor out of water while it's still running—the blade just roars with nothing to push against, and goes nowhere.

"Who knows," he went on, "maybe there's a kind of poetic justice in what happened to my snow crystals. Perhaps it was the same energy I wasted puttering around up here that ironically helped to give them life—a horrible, negative kind of life that breathes the dead gas in the air instead of oxygen."

"You weren't just puttering, Dad—don't say that. You know how much you did for cancer research!"

"That was a long time ago. No, I was puttering, Karen. And it was dangerous puttering, because I had the knowledge and the weapons to understand and use the forces I was playing with." He rose and walked towards the window.

"It's a tremendous force," he said. "And it's the same force, whether it's in us, in an atom of uranium, or in a crystal of snow. We can't stop it—all we can do is steer it. We have always a terrible alternative in our lives. Sometimes it doesn't take much pressure on the helm, one way or another, to make the difference to us, either as individuals, or as residents of a planet, between the making of a world, and the destruction of a world. . . ."

He broke off and turned towards them suddenly. David heard it too— a dull, rumbling sound that seemed to come from the air itself rather than from any particular direction. At the same time the floor had begun to tremble under their feet, and the dishes in the kitchen cupboard rattled.

David and Karen leaped to their feet, and for a moment the three stared at each other as the rumble increased to a roar.

"Another avalanche!" the professor cried. He ran across the room to the window on the mountain side. The roar reached a thundering crescendo.

[175]

Then came a series of muffled but tremendous booming thuds that sounded to David like the overlapping explosions of a salvo of artillery shells. Amidst the shrill crashing of fallen china, the wall of the mill facing the mountain lurched and sagged inwardly as a tremendous weight struck it from outside. Sparks flew from the grate as a sudden gust of wind flapped in the chimney, and glass tinkled and fell from the snow-blocked window as Cruickshank leaped back.

Then there was silence except for the whisper of snow, pouring like sand through the broken window. And in the comparative stillness they could hear a mournful singing sound, like wind in the eaves outside.

David and Karen ran to the windows in front. The bottom panes were dark where snow had flattened against them. And the snow was rising, slowly narrowing the rectangles of opaque blue light that came through the upper parts of the windows. "My God!" David cried. "It's burying us! Karen! The lights! Quick!"

The lights still worked. Just as Karen reached the switch, Nicolls burst through the door from the airway. But the unspoken question on his lips remained unasked as he saw the broken china on the floor, and the sagging wall.

"Jesus!" he said, and then, "Blips coming now every two seconds, and the needle's reversed direction. That means the source of current is now between our instruments on the bluff and us.

"In other words—that was it that just came over the cliff!"

29 . . .

Two POLICE CARS and a fire truck still stood in the Foss' dooryard at midnight. Flashlights bobbed back and forth over the dark, glassless windows of the first floor as firemen, and state troopers stepped over coils of hose, still searching the sodden house and grounds without knowing what it was they were looking for. Others went in and out of the barn, where some of Foss' cows still lowed restlessly in their stalls, while others, nearest the sliding door, had slumped down and lay grotesquely still, covered with stars of frost and surrounded by a faint mouldy smell.

But the searchlight of the fire truck was trained on the woods of the mountain slope behind the barn. Other searchlights, from army trucks parked in the fields, also played back and forth across the slope. In the glare of lights along the edge of the woods, a milling throng of helmeted soldiers, carrying flame throwers and fire-fighting water tanks, was gradually forming into a single line. Above the searchlights, Barker Mountain pulsed with its cold fire, throwing up streamers of angry, luminous cloud.

"Sure as hell like to know what happened," one of the soldiers said, sucking nervously on a last cigarette.

"Heard they got the two dames in the house out OK—found 'em hiding in a closet upstairs," another said. "Was you in the barn? Keerist what a stink! You coulda cut hamburgers right offa coupla them sonsabitches!"

"Whaddya mean! Them cows was froze, not fried!"

"Looked Goddam well-done to me!"

"Whaddya think we got up there—hot snow?"

"You take another look at that Goddam mountain and tell me if it ain't hot snow!"

"I just hope they get us off this Goddam mountain!" someone else said. No one had an answer to that, and just then a lieutenant ran along the line in front of them.

"OK, men, ready to move out!" he called. He blew a whistle and threw his arm forward. The line began to advance against its strange enemy. High on the slope some minutes later the first orange tongue from the flame throwers lashed out with a giant gasp, and a column of black smoke rose against the blue light of the mountain.

For a moment the four in the kitchen of the mill stared at the shattered window. The poisonous silver mist had already begun to billow into the room and sink towards the floor, where it crept forward under the heat that still came from the fireplace. Then Cruickshank seized a chair and set it under the window.

"John!" he cried breathlessly, "get down to the lab and watch that needle! When the time comes, open the door! You know what to do!" Nicolls ran for the stairs in the airway. Shielding his eyes from the mist with his arm, Cruickshank set one foot on the chair. "Blanket on the cot, Dave—quick!"

"Dad! What are you going to do?"

"Get back, Karen!" The professor was up on the chair, wobbling precariously, his arm still shielding his face, and the other groping blindly behind him. "Blanket! Hurry!" he repeated in a strangled voice. Then he seized the blanket David had pulled from the cot, and wadded it together, leaving his face exposed to the whirling mist as he did so. Ducking his head, he thrust the blanket blindly at the broken pane. But, as it struck the glass, he dropped it and clapped his hands to his face, half turning in the chair. Overbalanced, the chair fell backwards, the professor with it.

David heard Karen's cry behind him as he seized the blanket and righted the chair again. Burning needles seared his face and bare hands, and he kept his eyes tight shut as he thrust the blanket through the jagged glass. But this time it stayed and blocked the hole. Suddenly the mist in the room became a shower of settling sparks that winked out one by one.

[178]

In a moment David was beside Karen, helping her father up from the floor. Cruickshank, his glasses still remarkably intact, shook his head as if to clear it, then looked first at the window, then at David. "Good boy!" he said.

"Dad, are you all right?"

"Ankle—twisted my ankle, that's all." They helped him to his feet, but one leg gave under him as he put his weight on it. "Got to help me downstairs," he said, "no time to lose."

"You can't go downstairs," David said as they helped him to a chair well away from the broken window. "You're staying right here with Karen." He glanced at the window. The blanket was holding, and nothing was coming through. Cut off from its strange power, the snow on the floor had lost its glow, and the mist was already gone. "You're safe here now for the moment," he said. "Nicolls knows what to do downstairs and so do I."

"David, I must go down, I . . ." But he offered no resistance as they lowered him into the room's only armchair. His head fell forward on his chest, and he sat silent, breathing heavily. "You're right," he said finally, "but hurry! God help us if we've been wrong about this!"

Karen turned to him, her face chalk-pale. "David . . ." He took her shoulders and kissed her.

"Watch the window," he said. "If anything happens, yell as loud as you can!"

Downstairs he told Nicolls, who was watching the potentiometer, what had happened. "Good," the latter said without taking his eyes from the dial. "Glad he's out of it. I don't like this, David." He pointed to the dial. "It's gone crazy. I hitched up the receiver just outside . . ." He indicated the wire from the cellar window. "That's crazy too. Only thing I can figure is the damned thing's right outside now if it's ever going to be.

"If it isn't out there . . ." he looked at David with a fleeting sardonic smile, "it doesn't matter what we do. We can hold out for a while. But what's the use . . ."

"So we'd better open the door?" David felt a hollow, sick feeling in the pit of his stomach.

"Goddam right we'd better!" Nicolls had turned around and was staring at the crack between the bottom of the metal door and the sill where the wires to the potentiometer emerged. From the crack a spreading tentacle of white was advancing across the concrete floor, flowing almost like liquid. Even in the bright light of the overhead mercury lamps it glowed with its own brightness. Tiny diamond sparks danced in a halo around it.

"Stand by the hose!" was all Nicolls said. He took his position flat against the wall beside the metal door. David ran to the hose rack and dropped the heavy coils onto the floor. Then he poised himself with both hands on the wheel above the pipe. "OK," he said.

Nicolls swung the heavy latch-bar and let it drop free. Then he sprang back and ran to David's side.

With a harsh squeak, the door moved inward an inch or two and stopped, bright snow already whirling about the narrow aperture. Then the door swung inward and the snow burst in in a blinding avalanche. For a moment they could see the shining slope of the drift as it slithered into the room at incredible speed, striking and whirling around the end of the table like a tidal bore against a rocky promontory. Then the whole far end of the room was blotted out with shimmering, pulsing mist.

David's hands tightened on the valve wheel, but Nicolls gripped his arm. "Wait, not yet!" he cried. The mist was halfway across the room now and advancing slowly towards them. An advance tentacle of it rolled along the top of the table, curling exploringly around the potentiometer and the metal faucets in the sink, and then advancing again.

"My God! When!" David cried at last. Then he heard the squeal of the metal door again as it swung shut on its spring.

Nicolls struck his arm. "Now!"

David spun the wheel. The limp canvas hose stiffened and shot across the room. He heard the sudden roaring "whoosh" of water and the flat sticky sound of it striking something like wet mud. The mist retreated in a violent convulsion and whirled like live steam.

David tugged at the stiff hose, pulling it back towards him until he found the nozzle. Then he guided the stream slowly across the far end of the room. The stream, driven by the weight of the water in the pond, at first only punched holes in the mist which the swirling crystals quickly closed over. Then, suddenly, the mist was still, and became, as the mist in the kitchen upstairs had, only gleaming sparks that hung in the air like the afterglow of a Fourth of July rocket explosion. Then the sparks winked out and the mist was gone.

David saw the stream of his hose was splatting into a corner of a great mound of wet snow, deep enough to cover the entire far end of the table. The forces of the stream tore great fragments of slush away from the mound and hurled them against the wall, where they dissolved in churning froth.

"Shut it off!" Nicolls commanded. David dropped the nozzle and cranked the wheel until the stream became a trickle and ceased. Nicolls stepped forward through the inch-deep water that sloshed on the floor. He stood silent, looking at the mound of greyish, rotting snow. David heard steps on the stairs and turned. It was Karen.

"David, are you all right?"

"Yes, darling. You go back upstairs and tell your father I think we got it."

"Oh, Dave . . . thank God!" She stared for a moment at the inundated floor and the pale grey mass at the far end of the room, then turned and ran back up the stairs. David came up and stood beside Nicolls.

"Wasn't so hard after all," he said, looking down at what was left of the snow.

"Too easy." Nicolls brushed some of the wet snow off the top of the table. "It's dead all right, but it shouldn't have died so easily." He picked up a broom that was lying awash on the floor near the table and began poking at the mound. It broke away in wet chunks. "Nothing but snow," he said, "just like the stuff it surrounded itself with. Should have had more body."

He went to the metal door and, without hesitation, swung it open. From where he stood behind him, David could see the snow-covered stone steps. The snow that had slipped into the laboratory had left a great gap in the deep drifts sloping against the house. Through the gap, he could see the starlit sky behind the dark tops of the trees. The moon had apparently sunk low, and there was no blue shine now, either from the moon or snow. The luminous mist was gone, and the drifts lay cold and silent. "We must have got it," Nicolls said. "Wait here while I take a look up above."

David stood just inside the door, holding it open, and saw Nicolls' feet advance cautiously up the steps and disappear at the top. Then he heard the crash—an explosion of shattering glass, followed by a heavy thud that shook the wooden ceiling of the lab. There was a moment of silence. Then he heard Karen's shrill and terrible scream.

She screamed again as he reached her at the top of the stairs. Then, as he caught hold of her, she sank to her knees, sobbing hysterically, unable to speak. He looked through the doorway into the lighted kitchen and saw why she had screamed.

The whole window facing the mountain had crashed in, and a great shapeless something, wrapped in a luminous aura of blue mist, sprawled across the center of the floor, puffing itself up to nearly the height of a man at its center, and then collapsing again like a pricked bubble as it slipped and rolled further along the floor, making a gurgling, sucking sound, like tumbling jelly. It was moving slowly towards the doorway.

Behind it, Professor Cruickshank, half enveloped in the surrounding mist, was down on his knees, close to the sprawling shape, striking frenziedly at it with a kitchen chair, breathing in wheezing gasps between each stroke.

Plunging into the room, David crashed through the laboratory glassware as he circled the thing on the floor and seized the professor under the arms. The professor struggled vainly for a moment, and then dropped his chair as David dragged him away from the mist. He was almost limp as David got him to a far corner of the room and propped him against the wall where he sat inert, stunned and gasping. "Take it easy, Professor," he panted, scarcely able to breathe himself. Then he heard Karen scream again. He whirled around and realized too late what had happened. The white mass with its surrounding mist now completely blocked the doorway to the kitchen and was pouring through into the airway where Karen was.

For a second he stared in helpless, paralyzing horror. Then, guarding his eyes with his crossed arms, he ran headlong into the mist.

He tripped over something cold, wet, and resisting and fell forward into a suffocating whiteness. For a moment he was aware only of struggling blindly and desperately against something shapeless, but tangible, that was searing cold and felt like curdled milk against his bare hands. There was an inarticulate gurgling sound somewhere near him, like thick liquid bubbling, and a nauseous, fetid smell clogged his breath.

Then he was free and stumbling through mist that raked his eyes and the back of his throat. He felt a jarring wrench and blinding stab of pain in the side of his head as his momentum brought him crashing against the wall of the airway. For a moment, blackness swirled tentatively around him. Then, when he could see again, he raised himself to his hands and knees and looked for Karen.

In the dim, sickly light of the mist, he could see her standing against the wall under the stairs to the loft. Wide-eyed, and rigid as if frozen, she had flattened herself against the wall and was staring hypnotically at the thing on the floor in front of her.

Pulsing and undulating, and making a noise like escaping steam as bubbles of noxious vapor burst from its seething folds, the curdled mass had spread over almost the entire floor of the airway, and the mist was everywhere, choking and blinding.

In a single bound David had reached Karen's side. As he seized her by the arm to pull her towards him and carry her to safety, she turned to him with a mute beseeching look. Then her eyes closed and all the rigidity went out of her. He caught her just in time to keep her from falling forward into the bubbling whiteness.

There was nowhere to go now except back into the angle of the corner. He felt the bag of rock salt Dwight had tripped over under his feet, and half dragged Karen behind it. She stirred and whimpered as he braced himself against the corner of the wall, pressing her face against his shirt to keep it from the searing mist.

David knew suddenly that the bag of salt was a last and only temporary refuge. Beyond it was nothing but pulsing blue-whiteness now. In a moment of calm clarity his mind told him that this was the end. There could only be a few moments now before the terrible cold fire of the mist would do its work. Already he could only keep his eyes open for a matter of seconds, and his face, neck and hands felt as if they were being sprayed with scalding water. He had forgotten Cruickshank and Nicolls. There was no one left now but himself and Karen. He ripped open his shirt-front, trying to cover her face with the flap of it, and held her tighter.

There must be some way to strike back—some weapon—something to do but sit and wait until he was finished, and Karen too. There was no use trying to break through the thing in front of him as he had in the doorway—not carrying Karen. God! There must be something! It's only snow, he told himself, remembering his own and Karen's words. Only ordinary snow that melts . . . His free hand found the rough, cool surface of the bag of salt. Salt for the roads in winter—to melt the ice!

Propping the still-limp Karen in a corner, he struggled to his feet. The bag of salt took all his strength to lift, and the salt poured out of the open end as he raised it. With a mighty effort, he staggered into the whiteness and swung the open end of the bag violently forward. He heard the rush of pouring salt, and the thudding as it struck the jelly-like substance under the mist. Then, with his last strength, he hurled the remainder of the bag into the center of the whiteness and fell back against the wall alongside of Karen, shielding her face again.

The effect of the salt was almost instantaneous. The mist shuddered and retreated. The shapeless mass on the floor began to swell. An ominous bubbling sound rose from its soggy depths, and blue sparks shimmered upwards from its surface, turning slowly to green. The mass rose higher in a series of convulsive heavings. It swelled into a dome of great convex bubbles, and then the bubbles burst with an explosive sigh.

David felt Karen clinging to him now, as he watched in fascinated horror. As the bubbles burst, the whiteness, no longer luminous, withered and shrank into itself. In a few moments there was nothing left but a spattering of greyish slime, and a puddle of something that looked like wet chalk around the sodden burlap bag in the middle of the floor.

Coughing slightly from the pungent odor that suddenly filled the room, David looked down at Karen as he held her head in his lap. Her eyes were open, and she smiled as he looked at her. "It's all over, darling," he said, running his fingers over the undamaged smoothness of her cheek.

Then he saw Professor Cruickshank, supporting himself against the jamb of the kitchen door. Behind him stood Dr. Nicolls. Cruickshank had lost his glasses.

"David . . . thank God! Is Karen all right?"

"Yes, Dad, I'm all right." David helped her to her feet, and the professor embraced her as they came to the kitchen door. "I couldn't reach you in time because of my leg, David," he said over Karen's shoulder. "And you locked Nicolls outside when you let the laboratory door slam. I guess we weren't much help to you. Thank God you're all right! How did you do it?"

"Salt . . . the bag of salt."

"What made you think of that?"

David smiled weakly. "You said it was just ordinary snow!"

30 . . .

Dwight Heron, who had managed to get his car as far as the far side of the turnaround before he ran into deep snow, arrived a few minutes later. "I knew right away where you were when you didn't come to the house, Dave-boy," he said. "But I know you'll understand why I couldn't get here sooner."

"All quiet when you came up just now?" Nicolls asked.

Dwight nodded. "All moonlight and peaceful. Died down all of a sudden." He looked at the great hole in the kitchen wall where the window had been, then at Cruickshank, who was leaning on Nicolls for support, and David, who stood with his arm around Karen, his burned face shiny with grease. "What in the name of God happened up here?" he asked.

The four looked at each other in silence for a moment. Cruickshank smiled. "Just an experiment in emergency snow clearance," he said.

They all had to leave in Dwight's car because the professor's and David's, parked where the snow from the mountain had drifted around the corner of the mill, were buried too deep to move. Dwight and Nicolls helped the professor to the car, and David and Karen followed, leaving the mill dark behind them. In the turnaround they all stopped a moment and looked up in the direction of Barker Mountain. In the light of the setting moon, the spruces on top of the bluff were black and still. Above the bluff, the blue-black sky over the mountain was clear and full of stars.

"What was it, Nathan?" Dwight asked.

"What was it made of?" Cruickshank was still looking up at the bluff. "I can't tell you that. I can tell you it lived on what is poisonous to our kind of life, and that its life process created cold instead of warmth. But *what* it was—I guess we'll each have to find our own answer to that."

David and Karen lingered a little behind as the others climbed into the front seat of Dwight's car. "What's your answer, David?" she asked him. "What do you think it was?"

He took her in his arms, feeling her warmth against him in the coolness of the October night.

"I don't think there's any such thing," he said.